FAIR BARBARIAN

BY

FRANCES HODGSON BURNETT

Author of "That Lass o' Lowrie's," "Haworth's," "Louisiana," etc.

Copyright, 1880,
By FRANCES HODGSON BURNETT.

All rights reserved.

CONTENTS.

CHAPTER		PAGE
I.	Miss Octavia Bassett	5
II.	"An Investment, anyway"	14
III.	L'Argentville	24
IV.	Lady Theobald	31
V.	Lucia	42
VI.	Accidental	51
VII.	"I should like to see more of Slowbridge"	61
VIII.	Shares Looking Up	69
IX.	White Muslin	82
X.	Announcing Mr. Barold	90
XI.	A Slight Indiscretion	101
XII.	An Invitation	109
XIII.	Intentions	118
XIV.	A Clerical Visit	128
XV.	Superior Advantages	134
XVI.	Croquet	143
XVII.	Advantages	152
XVIII.	Contrast	166
XIX.	An Experiment	172

4 CONTENTS.

CHAPTER		PAGE
XX.	Peculiar to Nevada	183
XXI.	Lord Lansdowne	197
XXII.	"You have made it livelier"	207
XXIII.	"May I go?"	221
XXIV.	The Garden Party	230
XXV.	"Somebody else"	241
XXVI.	"Jack"	251

Woman of the West:
An Introduction to Frances Hodgson Burnett's *A Fair Barbarian*

Frances Hodgson Burnett is best known today for her children's novel *The Secret Garden*, but she published more than four dozen books during her lifetime, five of them bestsellers (Bixler, "Oral-Formulaic Training" 42). She wrote novels, short stories, articles, plays, a memoir, and many other children's books—including her runaway bestseller, *Little Lord Fauntleroy*. Her books were enormously popular, and Henry James, more than a little envious, once wrote to her to express his "joy at the thought of so many copies sold—my publisher's statement is usually *one* on alternate years . . ." (qtd. in Vivian Burnett 288). In addition to corresponding with James, Burnett also associated with other illustrious writers of her day. She visited Emily Dickinson (Thwaite 70), met Bret Harte on her honeymoon (Thwaite 44), and hosted an afternoon reception for Oscar Wilde (Vivian Burnett 113).

A FAIR BARBARIAN.

Mark Twain sent her a personally inscribed copy of *The Prince and the Pauper* (Thwaite 72), Oliver Wendell Holmes sent her an admiring letter (qtd. in Vivian Burnett 174-75), and Louisa May Alcott favorably reviewed her work (Thwaite 93).

Born in Manchester, England, in 1849, Burnett moved with her family to Tennessee when she was a teenager. After several years in the United States she revisited England, and for the rest of her life she divided her time evenly between the two countries, making a grand total of thirty-three Atlantic crossings in her seventy-five years (Thwaite 234). In many of her works she examines the differences between the two nations and their people, and her "international novels" were among her best and most popular. As Phyllis Bixler notes, "Because of *A Fair Barbarian*, *Little Lord Fauntleroy*, *The Shuttle*, and *T. Tembarom*, as well as because of her own highly publicized life as an Anglo-American, Burnett stands foremost among the writers of the era who interpreted for a popular audience the international themes of Henry James" (*Frances* 125).

Burnett's *A Fair Barbarian* "was her first extended expression of the internationalism

INTRODUCTION.

which was so characteristic of her life work" (Vivian Burnett 106). The novel is a charming comedy of manners in which a refreshingly vigorous heroine from the American West visits a modest English village whose name, Slowbridge, suggests the content of the story: young Octavia Bassett *slowly bridges* the gap between the freedom and independence of her native Nevada and the culture and tradition of Britain. The story first appeared in serial form in *Peterson's* and then *Scribner's* before being published as a book in 1881, when its author was thirty-one years old. "The neighbourhood are much amused by *A Fair Barbarian*," Emily Dickinson wrote in a letter dated March 1881, "and Emily's *Scribner* is perused by all the Boys and Girls—even the cynic Austin [her brother] confessed himself amused . . ." (qtd. in Thwaite 70).

The handful of serious critics who have paid any attention at all to this admittedly light, comic romp of a novel agree that it constitutes a spirited rejoinder to Henry James's portrayal of American womanhood in *Daisy Miller*.[1] Burnett's son, Vivian Burnett, disclaims any such conscious intention in his biography of his mother, a book titled *The Romantick Lady*:

> Henry James, with whom later in life Mrs. Burnett had a close friendship, had written his *Daisy Miller*, which was considered at the time to be the work of an expatriate, who did not do justice to the American girl. It was probably not at all in Mrs. Burnett's mind to "answer" Mr. James with her *Barbarian*, but she was considered, at least by some, as having done so with considerable success. (106)

Despite his ingenuous disclaimer, *A Fair Barbarian* constitutes part of an ongoing literary dialogue about the interaction of two cultures, those of the Old World and the New. In order to understand how Burnett's novel responds to James's work, it is necessary to understand the context in which she wrote—in particular, the popular response to James's *Daisy Miller*.

James first published the novella *Daisy Miller: A Study* in 1878 in the British periodical *Cornhill Magazine*, edited by Leslie Stephen (who today is perhaps best known as Virginia Woolf's father). The story was then published in a book in 1878 in America and 1879 in

INTRODUCTION.

Britain. The novella was so successful that in 1882 James adapted it for the theatre, but the play never achieved the same success.

The story is, for James especially, an unusually simple and straightforward one. An exquisitely pretty American girl named Daisy Miller travels with her family to Europe. Because she sees no need for a chaperone and socializes with the courier (who ought, of course, to be treated as an inferior), the Americans in Rome ostracize her. The story's focal character, American expatriate Frederick Winterbourne, initially sees her as merely naïve but eventually, after seeing her walking in the moonlight with the courier in the Coliseum, decides against her moral and sexual innocence. Daisy, wounded by Winterbourne's disdain, succumbs to malaria, then known as "Roman fever."

Perhaps not surprisingly, given its ambivalent portrayal of American womanhood, Daisy Miller created something of a stir. The manuscript had been rejected by *Lippincott's Magazine*, as James later admitted in his preface to the work, and the editor's

> ... absence of comment ... struck me at the time as rather grim—as, given the circumstances, requir-

> ing indeed some explanation: till a
> friend to whom I appealed for
> light, giving him the thing to read,
> declared it could only have passed
> with the Philadelphian critic for
> "an outrage on American girl-
> hood." ("On Daisy Miller" 369)

More than two decades later, James's friend William Dean Howells wrote, "It is pathetic to remember how *Daisy Miller* was received, or rather rejected, as an attack on American girlhood, and yet is so perfectly intelligible that it should have been taken so by Americans . . ." (Howells, "Mr." 113). Both Howells and the reviewer for the *New York Times* felt compelled to defend James's patriotism (Howells, "Mr." 113, Review 103).

Curiously (but perhaps not surprisingly), Howells notes a gender difference in readers' responses to Daisy: "The American man might have suffered her—perhaps more than suffered her even—but the American woman would [have] none of her. She fancied in the poor girl a libel of her nationality, almost a libel of her sex, and failed to seize her wilding charm, her flowerlike purity" ("Mr." 114). Howells was a bit blunter in private; in a letter to James

INTRODUCTION.

Russell Lowell, Howells wrote:

> ... Harry James waked up all the women with his *Daisy Miller*, the intention of which they misconceived, and there has been a vast discussion in which nobody felt very deeply, and everybody talked very loudly. The thing went so far that society almost divided itself into Daisy Millerites and anti-Daisy Millerites. (Howells, "To" 111-12)

About seven months after the story's publication, the *New York Times* published an editorial defending the novel and acknowledged, "There are many ladies in and around New York today who feel very indignant with Mr. James for his portrait of *Daisy Miller*, and declare that it is shameful to give foreigners so untrue a portrait of an American girl" ("[American]" 123).

Burnett may well have been one of the women readers who became so indignant. After all, Burnett had lived in a log cabin in the rural one-street town of New Market, Tennessee, from age fifteen until she was seventeen, and the family moved to a farmhouse in an even more isolated area outside Knoxville for several years after that (Thwaite 27-30). Burnett might easily have found the delicate scruples of James's Europeanized Americans excessive. As one contemporary reviewer pointed out, only New York and Boston society observed the kinds of rules which Daisy so blithely violated:

> Her conduct is without blemish, according to the rural American standard, and she knows no other. ... A few dozens, perhaps a few hundreds, of families in America have accepted the European theory of the necessity of surveillance for young ladies, but it is idle to say it has ever been accepted by the country at large. ("Contributor's Club" 111)

The heroine of *A Fair Barbarian* might easily strike female readers especially as a refreshing antidote to the neurasthenic Daisy, whose whole life collapses around her when she is cruelly misjudged by the coldly supercilious (and aptly named) Winterbourne.[2] As Phyllis Bixler observes,

> Like the young American women portrayed by James and Howells,

INTRODUCTION.

> Octavia sees no reason for abiding by the social restraints customary for European girls. Like Daisy Miller, she takes a moonlight walk alone with a young man, but unlike Daisy, who gets malaria and dies, Octavia does not suffer because of her freedom. (*Frances* 34)

Even Octavia's name suggests difference; as opposed to Daisy Miller, who was literally killed by Rome—specifically by *Roman* fever—Octavia bears the name of Roman emperor Caesar Augustus, who commanded the Roman empire during the life of Christ: "From her imperial name, Octavia, to her war-goddess jewelry, then, Hodgson Burnett's heroine is meant to be a conqueror, a leveler, 'a fair barbarian'" (Maher 148).

Daisy Miller is an Easterner; she comes to Europe from Schenectady, New York.[3] By contrast, Octavia Bassett comes to Slowbridge, England, from Bloody Gulch, Nevada.[4] Because the British regard the word "bloody" as profanity, she cannot even name her origin in polite society. The literal meaning of the place's name simply refers to the violence presumably more common in the "barbaric" American West than in, say, New England: "It was called that, in the first place, because a party of men were surprised and murdered there, while they were asleep in their camp at night," Octavia explains to her aunt (27). The name is interesting for other reasons as well; for example, it is reminiscent of Bret Harte's story "The Idyl of Red Gulch." In that story, a young schoolteacher's bitter discovery that her suitor has an illegitimate child confirms Eastern and European readers' suspicions of the sexual license of the lawless American West. If Octavia comes from such a place, her innocence, like poor Daisy's, is surely suspect.[5]

Her heritage is suspect as well. She is the daughter of a silver miner and a San Francisco actress (a profession then considered morally equivalent to a prostitute).[6] Because her mother died in childbirth at nineteen (21), Octavia was raised by her father: ". . . and once he had taken her to a Californian gold-diggers' camp, where she had been the only female member of the somewhat reckless community" (25). The gold jewelry Octavia receives from the miners further recalls the work of Bret Harte—specifically, the story "The Luck of

INTRODUCTION.

Roaring Camp," in which an orphaned child is given gifts and treated with a rough but genuine tenderness by the otherwise hardbitten men of a mining camp.

In contrast to this largely masculine Wild West mining camp, the Slowbridge setting owes a great deal to the quiet, largely female community of Cranford in Elizabeth Gaskell's novel of that name.[7] Octavia's timid, easily flustered aunt, Miss Belinda Bassett, greatly resembles Miss Matty Jenkyns of Gaskell's novel, and Lady Theobald takes over Mrs. Jamieson's role as social arbiter: "She had no hesitation in asking questions boldly; she considered it her privilege to do so: she had catechized Slowbridge for forty years, and meant to maintain her rights until Time played her the knave's trick of disabling her" (88).

A Fair Barbarian initially seems to follow the traditional heterosexual romance plot, but it gradually becomes apparent to the reader that Burnett's attention was instead focused on a different relationship—a strategy that she commonly adopted, according to her biographer:

> "I hate and detest love stories,"
> [Burnett] added, surprisingly per-

> haps for one who had written so many. "But it seems that you must have their grinning sentimental skeletons to hang your respectable humanity and drapery upon." It was undoubtedly true that Frances put no special value in many of her books on the love between man and woman, the sexual relationship. Many of the most strongly loving relationships are between mother and son, father and daughter, between sisters, between friends. (Thwaite 74)

Typically, then, the heart of *A Fair Barbarian* lies in the friendship that grows between the coolly confident Octavia and Lady Theobald's nineteen-year-old granddaughter, Lucia Gaston. Modest, simple Lucia is afraid of everything, in part because of the way in which she was raised by the stern and unforgiving Lady Theobald: "[Lucia] had been taught to view herself as rather a bad case, and to feel that she was far from being what her relatives had a right to expect" (210). Lucia echoes the narrator's judgment: "I am not clever, and

INTRODUCTION.

have been a sort of slave all my life, and have been scolded and blamed for what I could not help at all, until I have felt as if I must be a criminal" (111). Not surprisingly, her self-esteem has been nearly destroyed in the process of her upbringing. Mr. John Burmistone, the builder of the local mill, quietly and kindly encourages Lucia, and she finds herself strangely drawn to him. As she confesses to him, "I am nearly twenty, and it is time that I should learn to respect myself" (113).

Octavia also encourages Lucia to develop self-esteem—just as she encourages the timid, socially inept Rev. Alfred Poppleton to develop social confidence (140-41) and her easily flustered aunt to develop self-assurance. The values Octavia fosters—courage, independence, self-determination, and self-respect—are those traditionally associated with the mythic Old West: "Indeed, her frontier upbringing is a moral force to be reckoned with in Hodgson Burnett's novel: it is what empowers Octavia and enables her to reject the decided opinion of her social 'betters' and create her own happy ending" (Maher 152).

Octavia's differences are all attributed to her Western origin. Captain Francis Barold, for ex-

A FAIR BARBARIAN.

ample, suggests waspishly to the curate that Octavia's generosity (with her cash donations, as with her diamonds) may be "peculiar to Nevada" (196), while Lady Theobald is critical of Octavia's "Nevada frivolity and freedom of manners" (203). Octavia even jokes in a "Nevada way" (136). As Mrs. Burnham asks an annoyed Lady Theobald, "Who would have believed that she had come from Nevada to improve us?" (199).

At the same time Octavia, too, learns from Lucia (and, to a lesser degree, from her aunt, Belinda Bassett, and her suitor, Captain Barold) how to accommodate herself to the customs of the society in which she finds herself. She rather wistfully acknowledges to an uncomprehending and therefore dismissive Barold that she would like to be improved and that she admires Lucia (154-56); Lucia, on the other hand, admires Octavia's bravery and independence. For this reason, the two make a pact to help each other (175). Consequently, Octavia modifies the brashness of her dress and hairstyle (183-84), while the self-effacing Lucia finally confronts her grandmother and chooses to marry Mr. Burmistone despite Lady Theobald's objections.

Octavia's suitor, Captain Francis Barold, is

INTRODUCTION.

less fortunate. Octavia seems to recognize that in his selfishness he may be incapable of love. When he says, "I am not fond enough of any one to do any thing they ask me," her shrewd response is telling: "Octavia bestowed a long look upon him. 'Well,' she remarked, after a pause, 'I believe you are not. I wouldn't think so.'" (Burnett 138). The story suggests that he, like Sir Nigel Anstruthers in Burnett's later novel, *The Shuttle*, has the potential to become abusive. Lady Theobald terms him "just the man to please a girl,—good-looking, and with a fine, domineering air" (162). He is furious when "this little Nevada flirt" is kind to the curate (150), particularly when she finds the curate as amusing as she finds Barold (Burnett 190): "Her manners were not what he was accustomed to: she did not consider that all men were not to be regarded from the same point of view" (Burnett 217). His anger resembles the anger of the apparently murderous widower in Robert Browning's "My Last Duchess" who complains that his wife "ranked/ My gift of a nine-hundred-years-old name/ With anybody's gift" (lines 32-34, Browning 58-59).

Octavia's cool refusal of Barold's proposal owes something to Bessie Alden's rejection of Lord Lambeth in James's "An International

Episode" (Bixler 34), certainly, but it also has an even earlier and better known antecedent in the famous scene in *Pride and Prejudice* in which the wealthy and aristocratic Mr. Darcy proposes to Miss Elizabeth Bennet, whose relatives, like Octavia's, have the bad taste to engage in trade. When Octavia notes that "I was not the kind of girl you would have chosen of your own will" (249), she sounds very like the indignant Elizabeth talking to Darcy: "'I might as well enquire,' replied she, 'why with so evident a design of offending and insulting me, you chose to tell me that you liked me against your will, against your reason, and even against your character'" (Austen 222). Both suitors dwell rather inappropriately on the "obstacles" to the proposed unions.

The obstacles consist largely of considerations of class. Susan Naremore Maher points out that "class bigotry is the rotten center of Slowbridge," (149) and contends that Octavia's difference lies in her Western dismissal of the importance of such considerations: "Convention plays little part in the lives of Martin and Octavia Bassett; self-determination is the key to their happiness" (150). In several respects, *A Fair Barbarian* fits the definition of the English Western developed by James K. Folsom: The

INTRODUCTION.

West in this novel certainly represents economic opportunity, and the gold and silver seem surprisingly easy to find. Moreover, Octavia fits Folsom's description of "the hero of an English Western" as "a person in a position to enjoy the best of both worlds, who can use the opportunities of one as a means to make [her] way in the other" (135). But ultimately, of course, Octavia's allegiance is to the country of her birth, as Burnett's (carefully foreshadowed) surprise ending reveals. It was perhaps this ending which prompted the anonymous reviewer for the *Atlantic Monthly* to describe Burnett as "somewhat aggressively American in her choice of subject and treatment" ("Five" 861) and to ask, "Have we not our little revenge? Have we not a triumphant answer to the social sneer, Who knows an American lady?" ("Five" 862). Unlike James, Burnett clearly did not prompt her critics to defend her patriotism.

The literary dialogue did not end with Burnett's rejoinder to the all-too-easily vanquished Daisy, for *A Fair Barbarian* garnered at least two literary responses of its own, both of them short stories: "The Siege of London," by Henry James, and "The Adventure of the Noble Bachelor," by Sir Arthur Conan Doyle.

A FAIR BARBARIAN.

In the former, published in 1883, a British gentleman named Littlemore follows the career of an extraordinary American woman appropriately named Mrs. Headway, who is pronounced a "barbarian" more than half a dozen times throughout the course of the story (James, "Siege" 170, 184, 188, 209, 216, 225). As James observes in introducing her, "She was a genuine product of the wild West—a flower of the Pacific slope; ignorant, absurd, crude, but full of pluck and spirit, of natural intelligence and of a certain intermittent haphazard felicity of impulse" (James, "Siege" 170). James exaggerates the supposed sexual license of the American West to the point of comic caricature:

> She got divorces very easily, she was so taking in court. She had got one or two before from a man whose name he couldn't remember, and there was a legend that even these were not the first. She had been enormously divorced! When he first met her in California she called herself Mrs. Grenville, which he had been given to understand was not an appellation acquired by matri-

> mony, but her parental name, resumed after the dissolution of an unfortunate union. She had had these episodes —her unions were all unfortunate—and had borne half a dozen names. She was a charming woman, especially for New Mexico; but she had been divorced too often—it was a tax on one's credulity; she must have repudiated more husbands than she had married. (James, "Siege" 169).

In contrast to Daisy's relative disdain for (or at least ignorance of) "society," Nancy Headway is determined to enter it through marriage to a somewhat reluctant aristocrat. Here the cool self-assurance of Burnett's heroine—a quality repeatedly referred to in the novel itself as her characteristic *sang-froid* (65, 219, 220)—becomes sheer brazenness. Nancy Headway possesses none of Daisy's inscrutability—and none of her winning innocence. The West from which she comes lacks the moral energy of Octavia's Nevada; it seems instead to represent a wasteland of moral stupidity and sexual promiscuity.

Conan Doyle's heroine is less grotesque. The

redoubtable Hatty Doran, like Burnett's heroine, was raised by her father, grew up in a California mining camp, became an heiress, and received a proposal from a noble bachelor. Like Burnett's heroine, she, too, ultimately rejects British nobility for the love of an enterprising young American man with energy, sunburn, and sex appeal. The plot of this Sherlock Holmes story thus seems to be a direct descendant of *A Fair Barbarian*. One of the important clues in this mystery, interestingly enough, is a bit of American slang about "jumping a claim"; Burnett frequently used the jangling informality of American slang in her novels, particularly *The Shuttle* and *T. Tembarom*, to emphasize class differences. "The Adventure of the Noble Bachelor" was not one of Conan Doyle's favorites: "In a letter to a friend he put the story 'about the bottom of the list'" (qtd. in Conan Doyle 300), and Richard Foster has catalogued some of its more egregious implausibilities in a brief comic article for the *Baker Street Journal*. Nevertheless, it is fun and charming, particularly in its stereotyped portrayal of the American Westerners and the British aristocrat.

This conversation about international marriages continued, of course, with Burnett's own works, specifically *Little Lord Fauntleroy*, *The Shuttle*, and *T. Tembarom*, and with works by other writers. But Burnett had made her point already, disputing Jamesian semiotics even in the frothy, frivolous fairy tale of a *A Fair Barbarian* by having her self-possessed heroine complain irritably to Barold, "You think every thing means something, or is of some importance" (159). Octavia clearly does not. Burnett thus resists the kind of Jamesian interpretation Winterbourne constructs of Daisy Miller's character from Daisy's most casual, offhand, everyday choices about how to behave. Perhaps, as someone torn between two cultures, Burnett realized how easy it is to make the kind of mistake Daisy made and therefore in her works argued against too-facile assumptions about the intentions that prompted culturally objectionable behavior. *A Fair Barbarian*, then, can be read as a plea for intercultural patience and understanding.

Lisa Tyler
Sinclair Community College
Dayton, Ohio

THE FAIR BARBARIAN.

NOTES

1 See, for example, Phyllis Bixler *(Frances Hodgson Burnett*, 6, 33-34, 125) and Susan Naremore Maher (147).

2 If "neurasthenic" seems a harsh term to apply to the naïve Daisy, consider James's praise of Howells, whose genius, he believes, lies in the heroines he created:

> They have been American women in the scientific sense of the term, and the author, intensely American in the character of his talent, is probably never so spontaneous, so much himself, as when he represents the delicate, nervous, emancipated young woman begotten of our institutions and our climate, and equipped with a lovely face and an irritable moral consciousness. (James, Review 211)

Howells, then, was "the father of the American girl," the creator of the kind of character James was later to adopt as the central character of several of his greatest novels—among them *Portrait of a Lady* and *The Golden Bowl* (Eakin 84). Both men, drawing on a tradition

NOTES.

shared by such earlier writers as Harriet Beecher Stowe, wrote of a particular type of New England girl, one who coupled a Puritan heritage with the Emersonian ideal of self-culture (what we might term today self-fulfillment or the development of one's creative and moral potential). In doing so, they perhaps mistook the New England girl for the American girl and the New England heritage for the only American heritage worth writing about. Certainly these "delicate, nervous, emancipated young women" bear little resemblance to the hardier women of the American West.

3 Here I differ from Tristram P. Coffin, who describes Daisy Miller as "really little more than a western hero with parasol and bank account" (136).

4 Burnett establishes a similar contrast in her much lengthier 1907 novel *The Shuttle*. Rosalie and Bettina Vanderpoel in that novel both come from New York City, so the contrast is chronological rather than geographical. The sisters are separated by several years. When Rosalie, the older girl, marries Sir Nigel Anstruthers, she and her family are naïve about

what the scions of the Old World expect from their American brides and in-laws. When Bettin goes to rescue her older sister from her miserable marriage to an abusive aristocratic husband, she observes that the intervening years have permitted Americans to wisen up considerably.

5 Octavia's birthplace also suggests her universality; crudely put, it could be argued that all human beings come from a "bloody gulch," although the image is arguably misogynistic and grotesque.

6 Burnett's own sister, Edith, had gone to California with her husband to search for gold: "It was probably from Edith's letters that Frances had got the detail for Octavia's background in *A Fair Barbarian*" (Thwaite 149).

7 Perhaps the first critic to note Slowbridge's resemblance to Elizabeth Gaskell's Cranford in the novel of the same name was a contemporary anonymous reviewer for the *Atlantic Monthly* ("Five" 861). See also Thwaite (70), Bixler (126), and Maher (149).

Works Cited

"[American Mores and Daisy Miller.]" *New York Times* 4 June 1879: 4. Rpt. in *James's Daisy Miller: The Story, the Play, the Critics.* Ed. William T. Stafford. New York: Scribner's, 1964. 123-24.

Austen, Jane. *Pride and Prejudice.* 1813. New York: Penguin, 1972.

Bixler, Phyllis. *Frances Hodgson Burnett.* Boston: Twayne, 1984.

————. "The Oral-Formulaic Training of a Popular Fiction Writer: Frances Hodgson Burnett." *Journal of Popular Culture* 15 (Spring 1982): 42-52.

Browning, Robert. *Robert Browning's Poetry.* Ed. James F. Loucks. New York: Norton, 1979.

Burnett, Frances Hodgson. *A Fair Barbarian.* 1881. Moscow, Idaho: U of Idaho P, 1995.

Burnett, Vivian. *The Romanitc Lady (Frances Hodgson Burnett): The Life Story of an Imagination.* New York: Scribner's, 1927.

Coffin, Tristram P. "Daisy Miller: Western Hero." *Western Folklore* XVII (Oct.

1958): 273075. Rpt. in *James's Daisy Miller: The Story, the Play, the Critics*. Ed. William T. Stafford. New York: Scribner's, 1964. 136-37.

Conan Doyle, Sir Arthur. "The Adventure of the Noble Bachelor." *The Annotated Sherlock Holmes*. Ed. William S. Baring-Gould. 2 vols. New York: Clarkson, 1967. I: 281-300.

"The Contributor's Club." *Atlantic Monthly* 43 (February 1879): 253-62. Rpt. in *James's Daisy Miller: The Story, the Play, the Critics*. Ed. William T. Stafford. New York: Scribner's, 1964. 110-11.

Eakin, Paul John. *The New England Girl: Cultural Ideals in Hawthorne, Stowe, Howells, and James*. Athens: U of Georgia P, 1976.

"Five American Novels." *Atlantic Monthly* June 1881: 861-63.

Folsom, James K. "English Westerns." *The Western: A Collection of Critical Essays*. Ed. James K. Folsom. Englewood Cliffs, New Jersey: Prentice-Hall, 1979. 126-36.

Foster, Richard. "The Slippery Mr. Moulton, the Brazen Hatty Doran, and the

WORKS CITED.

Elusive Mr. Doran." *The Baker Street Journal* ns 24, 4 (Dec. 1974): 215-17.

Gaskell, Elizabeth. *Cranford*. 1853. New York: Penguin, 1994.

Harte, Bret. *The Writings of Bret Harte*. 20 vols. Boston: Houghton, Mifflin, and Company, 1896-1914.

Howells, William Dean. "To James Russell Lowell." 22 June 1879. *Life in Letters of William Dean Howells*. Ed. Mildred Howells. New York: Doubleday, 1928. I: 271. Rpt. in *James's Daisy Miller: The Story, the Play, the Critics*. Ed. William T. Stafford. New York: Scribner's, 1964. 111-12.

———. "Mr. James's Daisy Miller." *Heroines of Fiction*. New York: Harper & Brothers, 1901. 164-76. Rpt. in *James's Daisy Miller: The Story, the Play, the Critics*. Ed. William T. Stafford. New York: Scribner's, 1964. 112-14.

James, Henry. *Daisy Miller: A Study*. *Tales of Henry James*. Ed. Christof Wegelin. New York: Norton, 1984. 3-50.

———. "An International Episode." *Tales of Henry James*. Ed. Christof Wegelin. New York: Norton, 1984. 51-111.

———. "On *Daisy Miller*." *Tales of Henry*

James. Ed. Christof Wegelin. New York: Norton, 1984. 368-76.

———. Review of *A Foregone Conclusion*, by William Dean Howells. *Literary Reviews and Essays by Henry James: American, English, and French Literature*. Ed. Albert Mordell. New Haven, Connecticut: College and University P, 1957. 211-15.

———. "The Siege of London." *Americans and Europe: Selected Tales of Henry James*. Boston: Houghton Mifflin, 1965. 162-234.

Maher, Susan Naremore. "A Bridging of Two Cultures: Frances Hodgson Burnett and the Wild West." *Old West—New West: Centennial Essays*. Ed. Barbara Howard Meldrum. Moscow, Idaho: U of Idaho P, 1993. 146-53.

Review of *Daisy Miller: A Study*. *New York Times* 10 Nov. 1878: 10. Rpt. in *James's Daisy Miller: The Story, the Play, the Critics*. Ed. William T. Stafford. New York: Scribner's, 1964. 103-04.

Thwaite, Ann. *Waiting for the Party: The Life of Frances Hodgson Burnett*. New York: Scribner's. 1974.

A FAIR BARBARIAN.

CHAPTER I.

MISS OCTAVIA BASSETT.

SLOWBRIDGE had been shaken to its foundations.

It may as well be explained, however, at the outset, that it would not take much of a sensation to give Slowbridge a great shock. In the first place, Slowbridge was not used to sensations, and was used to going on the even and respectable tenor of its way, regarding the outside world with private distrust, if not with open disfavor. The new mills had been a trial to Slowbridge, — a sore trial. On being told of the owners' plan of building them, old Lady Theobald, who was the corner-stone of the social edifice of Slowbridge, was said, by a spectator, to have turned deathly pale with rage; and, on the first day of their being opened in working order, she had taken to her bed, and remained shut up in her darkened room for a week, refusing to see anybody, and even going so far as to send a scathing message to the curate of St. James, who called in fear and trembling, because he was afraid to stay away.

"With mills and mill-hands," her ladyship announced to Mr. Laurence, the mill-owner, when chance first threw them together, "with mills and mill-hands come murder, massacre, and mob law." And she said it so loud, and with so stern an air of conviction, that the two Misses Briarton, who were of a timorous and fearful nature, dropped their buttered muffins (it was at one of the tea-parties which were Slowbridge's only dissipation), and shuddered hysterically, feeling that their fate was sealed, and that they might, any night, find three masculine mill-hands secreted under their beds, with bludgeons. But as no massacres took place, and the mill-hands were pretty regular in their habits, and even went so far as to send their children to Lady Theobald's free school, and accepted the tracts left weekly at their doors, whether they could read or not, Slowbridge gradually recovered from the shock of finding itself forced to exist in close proximity to mills, and was just settling itself to sleep — the sleep of the just — again, when, as I have said, it was shaken to its foundations.

It was Miss Belinda Bassett who received the first shock. Miss Belinda Bassett was a decorous little maiden lady, who lived in a decorous little house on High Street (which was considered a very genteel street in Slowbridge). She had lived in the same house all her life, her father had lived in it, and so also had her grandfather. She had gone out, to take tea, from its doors two or three times a week, ever since she had been twenty; and she had had her little tea-parties in its front parlor as often as any other genteel Slowbridge entertainer. She had risen at seven, breakfasted at eight, dined at two, taken tea at five, and gone to bed at ten, with such regularity for fifty years, that to rise at eight, breakfast at nine, dine at three, and take tea at six, and go to bed at eleven, would, she was firmly convinced, be but "to fly in the face of Providence," as she put it, and sign her own death-warrant. Consequently, it is easy to imagine what a tremor and excitement seized her when, one afternoon, as she sat waiting for her tea, a coach from the Blue Lion dashed — or, at least, *almost* dashed — up to the front door, a young lady got out, and the next minute the handmaiden, Mary Anne, threw open the door of the parlor, announcing, without the least preface, —

"Your niece, mum, from 'Meriker."

Miss Belinda got up, feeling that her knees really trembled beneath her.

In Slowbridge, America was not approved of — in fact, was almost entirely ignored, as a country where, to quote Lady Theobald, "the laws were loose, and the prevailing sentiments revolutionary." It was not considered good taste to know Americans, — which was not unfortunate, as there were none to know; and Miss Belinda Bassett had always felt a delicacy in mentioning her only brother, who had emigrated to the United States in his youth, having first disgraced himself by the utterance of the blasphemous remark that "he wanted to get to a place where a fellow could stretch himself, and not be bullied by a lot of old tabbies." From the day of his departure, when he had left Miss Belinda bathed in tears of anguish, she had heard nothing of him; and here upon the threshold stood Mary Anne, with delighted eagerness in her countenance, repeating, —

"Your niece, mum, from 'Meriker!"

And, with the words, her niece entered.

Miss Belinda put her hand to her heart.

The young lady thus announced was the prettiest, and at the same time the most extraordinary-looking, young lady she had ever seen in her life. Slowbridge contained nothing approaching this niece. Her dress was so very stylish that it was quite startling in its effect; her forehead was covered down to her large, pretty eyes themselves, with curls of yellow-brown hair; and her slender throat was swathed round and round with a grand scarf of black lace.

She made a step forward, and then stopped, looking at Miss Belinda. Her eyes suddenly, to Miss Belinda's amazement, filled with tears.

"Didn't you," she said, — "oh, dear! *Didn't* you get the letter?"

"The — the letter!" faltered Miss Belinda. "What letter, my — my dear?"

"Pa's," was the answer. "Oh! I see you didn't."

And she sank into the nearest chair, putting her hands up to her face, and beginning to cry outright.

"I — am Octavia B-bassett," she said. "We were coming to surp-prise you, and travel in Europe; but the mines went wrong, and p-pa was obliged to go back to Nevada."

"The mines?" gasped Miss Belinda.

"S-silver-mines," wept Octavia. "And we had scarcely landed when Piper cabled, and pa had to turn back. It was something about shares, and he may have lost his last dollar."

Miss Belinda sank into a chair herself.

"Mary Anne," she said faintly, "bring me a glass of water."

Her tone was such that Octavia removed her handkerchief from her eyes, and sat up to examine her.

"Are you frightened?" she asked, in some alarm.

Miss Belinda took a sip of the water brought by her handmaiden, replaced the glass upon the salver, and shook her head deprecatingly.

"Not exactly frightened, my dear," she said, "but so amazed that I find it difficult to — to collect myself."

Octavia put up her handkerchief again to wipe away a sudden new gush of tears.

"If shares intended to go down," she said, "I don't see why they couldn't go down before we started, instead of waiting until we got over here, and then spoiling every thing."

"Providence, my dear" — began Miss Belinda.

But she was interrupted by the re-entrance of Mary Anne.

"The man from the Lion, mum, wants to know what's to be done with the trunks. There's six of 'em, an' they're all that 'eavy as he says he wouldn't lift one alone for ten shilling."

"Six!" exclaimed Miss Belinda. "Whose are they?"

"Mine," replied Octavia. "Wait a minute. I'll go out to him."

Miss Belinda was astounded afresh by the alacrity with which her niece seemed to forget her troubles, and rise to the occasion. The girl ran to the front door as if she was quite used to directing her own affairs, and began to issue her orders.

"You will have to get another man," she said. "You might have known that. Go and get one somewhere."

And when the man went off, grumbling a little, and evidently rather at a loss before such peremptory coolness, she turned to Miss Belinda.

"Where must he put them? she asked.

It did not seem to have occurred to her once that her identity might be doubted, and some slight obstacles arise before her.

"I am afraid," faltered Miss Belinda, "that five of them will have to be put in the attic."

And in fifteen minutes five of them *were* put into the attic, and the sixth — the biggest of all — stood in the trim little spare chamber, and pretty Miss Octavia had sunk into a puffy little chintz-covered easy-chair, while her newly found relative stood before her, making the most laudable efforts to recover her equilibrium, and not to feel as if her head were spinning round and round.

CHAPTER II.

"AN INVESTMENT, ANYWAY."

THE natural result of these efforts was, that Miss Belinda was moved to shed a few tears.

"I hope you will excuse my being too startled to say I was glad to see you," she said. "I have not seen my brother for thirty years, and I was very fond of him."

"He said you were," answered Octavia; "and he was very fond of you too. He didn't write to you, because he made up his mind not to let you hear from him until he was a rich man; and then he thought he would wait until he could come home, and surprise you. He was awfully disappointed when he had to go back without seeing you."

"Poor, dear Martin!" wept Miss Belinda gently. "Such a journey!"

Octavia opened her charming eyes in surprise.

"Oh, he'll come back again!" she said.

"And he doesn't mind the journey. The journey is nothing, you know."

"Nothing!" echoed Miss Belinda. "A voyage across the Atlantic nothing? When one thinks of the danger, my dear" —

Octavia's eyes opened a shade wider.

"We have made the trip to the States, across the Isthmus, twelve times, and that takes a month," she remarked. "So we don't think ten days much."

"Twelve times!" said Miss Belinda, quite appalled. "Dear, dear, dear!"

And for some moments she could do nothing but look at her young relative in doubtful wonder, shaking her head with actual sadness.

But she finally recovered herself, with a little start.

"What am I thinking of," she exclaimed remorsefully, "to let you sit here in this way? Pray excuse me, my dear. You see I am so upset."

She left her chair in a great hurry, and proceeded to embrace her young guest tenderly, though with a little timorousness. The young lady submitted to the caress with much composure.

"Did I upset you?" she inquired calmly.

The fact was, that she could not see why the simple advent of a relative from Nevada should seem to have the effect of an earthquake, and result in tremor, confusion, and tears. It was true, she herself had shed a tear or so, but then her troubles had been accumulating for several days; and she had not felt confused yet.

When Miss Belinda went down-stairs to superintend Mary Anne in the tea-making, and left her guest alone, that young person glanced about her with a rather dubious expression.

"It is a queer, nice little place," she said. "But I don't wonder that pa emigrated, if they always get into such a flurry about little things. I might have been a ghost."

Then she proceeded to unlock the big trunk, and attire herself.

Down-stairs, Miss Belinda was wavering between the kitchen and the parlor, in a kindly flutter.

"Toast some muffins, Mary Anne, and bring in the cold roast fowl," she said. "And I will put out some strawberry-jam, and some of the preserved ginger. Dear me! Just to think how fond of preserved ginger poor Martin was, and how little of it he was allowed to eat! There really seems a special Providence in my having such a nice stock of it in the house when his daughter comes home."

In the course of half an hour every thing was in readiness; and then Mary Anne, who had been sent up-stairs to announce the fact, came down in a most remarkable state of delighted agitation, suppressed ecstasy and amazement exclaiming aloud in every feature.

"She's dressed, mum," she announced, "an' 'll be down immediate," and retired to a shadowy corner of the kitchen passage, that she might lie in wait unobserved.

Miss Belinda, sitting behind the tea-service, heard a soft, flowing, silken rustle sweeping down the staircase, and across the hall, and then her niece entered.

"Don't you think I've dressed pretty quick?" she said, and swept across the little parlor, and sat down in her place, with the calmest and most unconscious air in the world.

There was in Slowbridge but one dressmaking establishment. The head of the establishment — Miss Letitia Chickie — designed the costumes of every woman in Slowbridge, from Lady Theobald down. There were legends that she received her patterns from London, and modified them to suit the Slowbridge taste. Possibly this was true; but in that case her labors as modifier must have been severe indeed, since they were so far modified as to be altogether unrecognizable when they left Miss Chickie's establishment, and were borne home in triumph to the houses of her patrons. The taste of Slowbridge was quiet, — upon this Slowbridge prided itself especially, — and, at the same time, tended toward economy. When gores came into fashion, Slowbridge clung firmly, and with some pride, to substantial breadths, which did not cut good silk into useless strips which could not be utilized in after-time; and it was only when, after a visit to London, Lady Theobald walked into St. James's one Sunday with two gores on each side, that Miss Chickie regretfully put scissors into her first breadth.

AN INVESTMENT, ANYWAY. 19

Each matronly member of good society possessed a substantial silk gown of some sober color, which gown, having done duty at two years' tea-parties, descended to the grade of "second-best," and so descended, year by year, until it disappeared into the dim distance of the past. The young ladies had their white muslins and natural flowers; which latter decorations invariably collapsed in the course of the evening, and were worn during the latter half of any festive occasion in a flabby and hopeless condition. Miss Chickie made the muslins, festooning and adorning them after designs emanating from her fertile imagination. If they were a little short in the body, and not very generously proportioned in the matter of train, there was no rival establishment to sneer, and Miss Chickie had it all her own way; and, at least, it could never be said that Slowbridge was vulgar or overdressed.

Judge, then, of Miss Belinda Bassett's condition of mind when her fair relative took her seat before her.

What the material of her niece's dress was, Miss Belinda could not have told. It was a silken and soft fabric of a pale blue color; it clung to the slender, lissome young figure like a glove; a fan-like train of great length almost covered the hearth-rug; there were plaitings and frillings all over it, and yards of delicate satin ribbon cut into loops in the most recklessly extravagant manner.

Miss Belinda saw all this at the first glance, as Mary Anne had seen it, and, like Mary Anne, lost her breath; but, on her second glance, she saw something more. On the pretty, slight hands were three wonderful, sparkling rings, composed of diamonds set in clusters: there were great solitaires in the neat little ears, and the thickly-plaited lace at the throat was fastened by a diamond clasp.

"My dear," said Miss Belinda, clutching helplessly at the teapot, "are you — surely it is a — a little dangerous to wear such — such priceless ornaments on ordinary occasions."

Octavia stared at her for a moment uncomprehendingly.

"Your jewels, I mean, my love," fluttered Miss Belinda. "Surely you don't wear them

AN INVESTMENT, ANYWAY. 21

often. I declare, it quite frightens me to think of having such things in the house."

"Does it?" said Octavia. "That's queer."

And she looked puzzled for a moment again.

Then she glanced down at her rings.

"I nearly always wear these," she remarked. "Father gave them to me. He gave me one each birthday for three years. He says diamonds are an investment, anyway, and I might as well have them. These," touching the ear-rings and clasp, "were given to my mother when she was on the stage. A lot of people clubbed together, and bought them for her. She was a great favorite."

Miss Belinda made another clutch at the handle of the teapot.

"Your mother!" she exclaimed faintly. "On the — did you say, on the " —

"Stage," answered Octavia. "San Francisco. Father married her there. She was awfully pretty. I don't remember her. She died when I was born. She was only nineteen."

The utter calmness, and freedom from embarrassment, with which these announcements were made, almost shook Miss Belinda's faith in her own identity. Strange to say, until this moment she had scarcely given a thought to her brother's wife; and to find herself sitting in her own genteel little parlor, behind her own tea-service, with her hand upon her own teapot, hearing that this wife had been a young person who had been "a great favorite" upon the stage, in a region peopled, as she had been led to suppose, by gold-diggers and escaped convicts, was almost too much for her to support herself under. But she did support herself bravely, when she had time to rally.

"Help yourself to some fowl, my dear," she said hospitably, even though very faintly indeed, "and take a muffin."

Octavia did so, her over-splendid hands flashing in the light as she moved them.

"American girls always have more things than English girls," she observed, with admirable coolness. "They dress more. I have been told so by girls who have been in Europe. And I have more things than most American girls. Father had more money than most people; that was one reason; and he spoiled me, I suppose. He had no one else to give things to, and he said I should have every thing I took a fancy to. He often laughed at me for buying things, but he never said I shouldn't buy them."

"He was always generous," sighed Miss Belinda. "Poor, dear Martin!"

Octavia scarcely entered into the spirit of this mournful sympathy. She was fond of her father, but her recollections of him were not pathetic or sentimental.

"He took me with him wherever he went," she proceeded. "And we had a teacher from the States, who travelled with us sometimes. He never sent me away from him. I wouldn't have gone if he had wanted to send me — and he didn't want to," she added, with a satisfied little laugh.

CHAPTER III.

L'ARGENTVILLE.

Miss Belinda sat, looking at her niece, with a sense of being at once stunned and fascinated. To see a creature so young, so pretty, so luxuriously splendid, and at the same time so simply and completely at ease with herself and her surroundings, was a revelation quite beyond her comprehension. The best-bred and nicest girls Slowbridge could produce were apt to look a trifle conscious and timid when they found themselves attired in the white muslin and floral decorations; but this slender creature sat in her gorgeous attire, her train flowing over the modest carpet, her rings flashing, her ear-pendants twinkling, apparently entirely oblivious of, or indifferent to, the fact that all her belongings were sufficiently out of place to be startling beyond measure.

Her chief characteristic, however, seemed

to be her excessive frankness. She did not hesitate at all to make the most remarkable statements concerning her own and her father's past career. She made them, too, as if there was nothing unusual about them. Twice, in her childhood, a luckless speculation had left her father penniless; and once he had taken her to a Californian gold-diggers' camp, where she had been the only female member of the somewhat reckless community.

"But they were pretty good-natured, and made a pet of me," she said; "and we did not stay very long. Father had a stroke of luck, and we went away. I was sorry when we had to go, and so were the men. They made me a present of a set of jewelry made out of the gold they had got themselves. There is a breastpin like a breastplate, and a necklace like a dog-collar: the bracelets tire my arms, and the ear-rings pull my ears; but I wear them sometimes — gold girdle and all."

"Did I," inquired Miss Belinda timidly, "did I understand you to say, my dear, that your father's business was in some way connected with silver-mining?"

"It *is* silver-mining," was the response. "He owns some mines, you know" —

"Owns?" said Miss Belinda, much fluttered; "owns some silver-mines? He must be a very rich man, — a very rich man. I declare, it quite takes my breath away."

"Oh! he is rich," said Octavia; "awfully rich sometimes. And then again he isn't. Shares go up, you know; and then they go down, and you don't seem to have any thing. But father generally comes out right, because he is lucky, and knows how to manage."

"But — but how uncertain!" gasped Miss Belinda: "I should be perfectly miserable. Poor, dear Mar" —

"Oh, no, you wouldn't!" said Octavia: "you'd get used to it, and wouldn't mind much, particularly if you were lucky as father is. There is every thing in being lucky, and knowing how to manage. When we first went to Bloody Gulch" —

"My dear!" cried Miss Belinda, aghast. "I — I beg of you" —

Octavia stopped short: she gazed at Miss Belinda in bewilderment, as she had done several times before.

"Is any thing the matter?" she inquired placidly.

"My dear love," explained Miss Belinda innocently, determined at least to do her duty, "it is not customary in — in Slowbridge, — in fact, I think I may say in England, — to use such — such exceedingly — I don't want to wound your feelings, my dear, — but such exceedingly strong expressions! I refer, my dear, to the one which began with a B. It is really considered profane, as well as dreadful beyond measure."

"'The one which began with a B,'" repeated Octavia, still staring at her. "That is the name of a place; but I didn't name it, you know. It was called that, in the first place, because a party of men were surprised and murdered there, while they were asleep in their camp at night. It isn't a very nice name, of course, but I'm not responsible for it; and besides, now the place is growing, they are going to call it Athens or Magnolia Vale. They tried L'Argentville for a while; but people would call it Lodginville, and nobody liked it."

"I trust you never lived there," said Miss

Belinda. "I beg your pardon for being so horrified, but I really could not refrain from starting when you spoke; and I cannot help hoping you never lived there."

"I live there now, when I am at home," Octavia replied. "The mines are there; and father has built a house, and had the furniture brought on from New York."

Miss Belinda tried not to shudder, but almost failed.

"Won't you take another muffin, my love?" she said, with a sigh. "Do take another muffin."

"No, thank you," answered Octavia; and it must be confessed that she looked a little bored, as she leaned back in her chair, and glanced down at the train of her dress. It seemed to her that her simplest statement or remark created a sensation.

Having at last risen from the tea-table, she wandered to the window, and stood there, looking out at Miss Belinda's flower-garden. It was quite a pretty flower-garden, and a good-sized one considering the dimensions of the house. There were an oval grass-plot, divers gravel paths, heart and diamond shaped beds aglow with brilliant annuals, a great many rose-bushes, several laburnums and lilacs, and a trim hedge of holly surrounding it.

"I think I should like to go out and walk around there," remarked Octavia, smothering a little yawn behind her hand. "Suppose we go — if you don't care."

"Certainly, my dear," assented Miss Belinda. "But perhaps," with a delicately dubious glance at her attire, "you would like to make some little alteration in your dress — to put something a little — dark over it."

Octavia glanced down also.

"Oh, no!" she replied: "it will do well enough. I will throw a scarf over my head, though; not because I need it," unblushingly, "but because I have a lace one that is very becoming."

She went up to her room for the article in question, and in three minutes was down again. When she first caught sight of her, Miss Belinda found herself obliged to clear her throat quite suddenly. What Slowbridge would think of seeing such a toilet in her front garden, upon an ordinary occasion, she could not imagine. The scarf truly was becoming. It was a long affair of rich white lace, and was thrown over the girl's head, wound around her throat, and the ends tossed over her shoulders, with the most picturesque air of carelessness in the world.

"You look quite like a bride, my dear Octavia," said Miss Belinda. "We are scarcely used to such things in Slowbridge."

But Octavia only laughed a little.

"I am going to get some pink roses, and fasten the ends with them, when we get into the garden," she said.

She stopped for this purpose at the first rose-bush they reached. She gathered half a dozen slender-stemmed, heavy-headed buds, and, having fastened the lace with some, was carelessly placing the rest at her waist, when Miss Belinda started violently.

CHAPTER IV.

LADY THEOBALD.

"OH, dear!" she exclaimed nervously, "there is Lady Theobald."

Lady Theobald, having been making calls of state, was returning home rather later than usual, when, in driving up High Street, her eye fell upon Miss Bassett's garden. She put up her eyeglasses, and gazed through them severely; then she issued a mandate to her coachman.

"Dobson," she said, "drive more slowly."

She could not believe the evidence of her own eyeglasses. In Miss Bassett's garden she saw a tall girl, "dressed," as she put it, "like an actress," her delicate dress trailing upon the grass, a white lace scarf about her head and shoulders, roses in that scarf, roses at her waist.

"Good heavens!" she exclaimed: "is Belinda Bassett giving a party, without so much as mentioning it to *me?*"

Then she issued another mandate.

"Dobson," she said, "drive faster, and drive me to Miss Bassett's."

Miss Belinda came out to the gate to meet her, quaking inwardly. Octavia simply turned slightly where she stood, and looked at her ladyship, without any pretence of concealing her curiosity.

Lady Theobald bent forward in her landau.

"Belinda," she said, "how do you do? I did not know you intended to introduce garden-parties into Slowbridge."

"Dear Lady Theobald"— began Miss Belinda.

"Who is that young person?" demanded her ladyship.

"She is poor dear Martin's daughter," answered Miss Belinda. "She arrived to-day — from Nevada, where — where it appears Martin has been very fortunate, and owns a great many silver-mines"—

"A 'great many' silver-mines!" cried Lady Theobald. "Are you mad, Belinda Bassett? I am ashamed of you. At your time of life too!"

Miss Belinda almost shed tears.

"She said 'some silver-mines,' I am sure," she faltered; "for I remember how astonished and bewildered I was. The fact is, that she is such a very singular girl, and has told me so many wonderful things, in the strangest, cool way, that I am quite uncertain of myself. Murderers, and gold-diggers, and silver-mines, and camps full of men without women, making presents of gold girdles and dog-collars, and ear-rings that drag your ears down. It is enough to upset any one."

"I should think so," responded her ladyship. "Open the carriage-door, Belinda, and let me get out."

She felt that this matter must be inquired into at once, and not allowed to go too far. She had ruled Slowbridge too long to allow such innovations to remain uninvestigated. She would not be likely to be "upset," at least. She descended from her landau, with her most rigorous air. Her stout, rich black *moire-antique* gown rustled severely; the yellow ostrich feather in her bonnet waved majestically. (Being a brunette, and Lady Theobald, she wore yellow.) As she tramped up the gravel walk, she held up her dress with both hands, as an example to vulgar and reckless young people who wore trains and left them to take care of themselves.

Octavia was arranging afresh the bunch of long-stemmed, swaying buds at her waist, and she was giving all her attention to her task when her visitor first addressed her.

"How do you do?" remarked her ladyship, in a fine, deep voice.

Miss Belinda followed her meekly.

"Octavia," she explained, "this is Lady Theobald, whom you will be very glad to know. She knew your father."

"Yes," returned my lady, "years ago. He has had time to improve since then. How do you do?"

Octavia's limpid eyes rested serenely upon her.

"How do you do?" she said, rather indifferently.

"You are from Nevada?" asked Lady Theobald.

"Yes."

"It is not long since you left there?"

Octavia smiled faintly.

"Do I look like that?" she inquired.

"Like what?" said my lady.

"As if I had not long lived in a civilized place. I dare say I do, because it is true that I haven't."

"You don't look like an English girl," remarked her ladyship.

Octavia smiled again. She looked at the yellow feather and stout *moire antique* dress, but quite as if by accident, and without any mental deduction; then she glanced at the rosebuds in her hand.

"I suppose I ought to be sorry for that," she observed. "I dare say I shall be in time — when I have been longer away from Nevada."

"I must confess," admitted her ladyship, and evidently without the least regret or embarrassment, "I must confess that I don't know where Nevada is."

"It isn't in Europe," replied Octavia, with a soft, light laugh. "You know that, don't you?"

The words themselves sounded to Lady Theobald like the most outrageous impudence; but when she looked at the pretty, lovelock-shaded face, she was staggered —

the look it wore was such a very innocent and undisturbed one. At the moment, the only solution to be reached seemed to be that this was the style of young people in Nevada, and that it was ignorance and not insolence she had to do battle with — which, indeed, was partially true.

"I have not had any occasion to inquire where it is situated, so far," she responded firmly. "It is not so necessary for English people to know America as it is for Americans to know England."

"Isn't it?" said Octavia, without any great show of interest. "Why not?"

"For — for a great many reasons it would be fatiguing to explain," she answered courageously. "How is your father?"

"He is very sea-sick now," was the smiling answer, — "deadly sea-sick. He has been out just twenty-four hours."

"Out? What does that mean?"

"Out on the Atlantic. He was called back suddenly, and obliged to leave me. That is why I came here alone."

"Pray do come into the parlor, and sit down, dear Lady Theobald," ventured Miss Belinda. "Octavia" —

"Don't you think it is nicer out here?" said Octavia.

"My dear," answered Miss Belinda. "Lady Theobald "— She was really quite shocked.

"Ah!" interposed Octavia. "I only thought it was cooler."

She preceded them, without seeming to be at all conscious that she was taking the lead.

"You had better pick up your dress, Miss Octavia," said Lady Theobald rather acidly.

The girl glanced over her shoulder at the length of train sweeping the path, but she made no movement toward picking it up.

"It is too much trouble, and one has to duck down so," she said. "It is bad enough to have to keep doing it when one is on the street. Besides, they would never wear out if one took too much care of them."

When they went into the parlor, and sat down, Lady Theobald made excellent use of her time, and managed to hear again all that had tried and bewildered Miss Belinda. She had no hesitation in asking questions boldly; she considered it her privilege to do so: she had catechised Slowbridge for forty years, and meant to maintain her rights until Time played her the knave's trick of disabling her.

In half an hour she had heard about the silver-mines, the gold-diggers, and L'Argentville; she knew that Martin Bassett was a millionnaire, if the news he had heard had not left him penniless; that he would return to England, and visit Slowbridge, as soon as his affairs were settled. The precarious condition of his finances did not seem to cause Octavia much concern. She had asked no questions when he went away, and seemed quite at ease regarding the future.

"People will always lend him money, and then he is lucky with it," she said.

She bore the catechising very well. Her replies were frequently rather trying to her interlocutor, but she never seemed troubled, or ashamed of any thing she had to say; and she wore, from first to last, that inscrutably innocent and indifferent little air.

She did not even show confusion when Lady Theobald, on going away, made her farewell comment: —

"You are a very fortunate girl to own such jewels," she said, glancing critically at the diamonds in her ears; "but if you take my advice, my dear, you will put them away, and save them until you are a married woman. It is not customary, on this side of the water, for young girls to wear such things — particularly on ordinary occasions. People will think you are odd."

"It is not exactly customary in America," replied Octavia, with her undisturbed smile. "There are not many girls who have such things. Perhaps they would wear them if they had them. I don't care a very great deal about them, but I mean to wear them."

Lady Theobald went away in a dudgeon.

"You will have to exercise your authority, Belinda, and *make* her put them away," she said to Miss Bassett. "It is absurd — besides being atrocious."

"Make her!" faltered Miss Bassett.

"Yes, 'make her' — though I see you will have your hands full. I never heard such romancing stories in my life. It is just what one might expect from your brother Martin."

When Miss Bassett returned, Octavia was standing before the window, watching the carriage drive away, and playing absently with one of her ear-rings as she did so.

"What an old fright she is!" was her first guileless remark.

Miss Belinda quite bridled.

"My dear," she said, with dignity, "no one in Slowbridge would think of applying such a phrase to Lady Theobald."

Octavia turned around, and looked at her.

"But don't you think she is one?" she exclaimed. "Perhaps I oughtn't to have said it; but you know we haven't any thing as bad as that, even out in Nevada — really!"

"My dear," said Miss Belinda, "different countries contain different people; and in Slowbridge *we* have our standards," — her best cap trembling a little with her repressed excitement.

But Octavia did not appear overwhelmed by the existence of the standards in question. She turned to the window again.

"Well, anyway," she said, "I think it was pretty cool in her to order me to take off my diamonds, and save them until I was married. How does she know whether I mean to be married, or not? I don't know that I care about it."

CHAPTER V.

LUCIA.

IN this manner Slowbridge received the shock which shook it to its foundations, and it was a shock from which it did not recover for some time. Before ten o'clock the next morning, everybody knew of the arrival of Martin Bassett's daughter.

The very boarding-school (Miss Pilcher's select seminary for young ladies, "combining the comforts of a home," as the circular said, "with all the advantages of genteel education") was on fire with it, highly colored versions of the stories told being circulated from the "first class" downward, even taking the form of an Indian princess, tattooed blue, and with difficulty restrained from indulging in war-whoops, — which last feature so alarmed little Miss Bigbee, aged seven, that she retired in fear and trembling, and shed tears under the bedclothes; her terror and anguish being much increased by the stirring recitals of scalping-stories by pretty Miss Phipps, of the first class — a young person who possessed a vivid imagination, and delighted in romances of a tragic turn.

"I have not the slightest doubt," said Miss Phipps, "that when she is at home she lives in a wampum."

"What is a wampum?" inquired one of her admiring audience.

"A tent," replied Miss Phipps, with some impatience. "I should think any goose would know that. It is a kind of tent hung with scalps and — and — moccasins, and — lariats — and things of that sort."

"I don't believe that is the right name for it," put in Miss Smith, who was a pert member of the third class.

"Ah!" commented Miss Phipps, "that was Miss Smith who spoke, of course. We may always expect information from Miss Smith. I trust that I may be allowed to say that I *think* I *have* a brother" —

"He doesn't know much about it, if he calls a wigwam a wampum," interposed Miss

Smith, with still greater pertness. "I have a brother who knows better than that, if I am only in the third class."

For a moment Miss Phipps appeared to be meditating. Perhaps she was a trifle discomfited; but she recovered herself after a brief pause, and returned to the charge.

"Well," she remarked, "perhaps it is a wigwam. Who cares if it is? And at any rate, whatever it is, I haven't the slightest doubt that she lives in one."

This comparatively tame version was, however, entirely discarded when the diamonds and silver-mines began to figure more largely in the reports. Certainly, pretty, overdressed, jewel-bedecked Octavia gave Slowbridge abundant cause for excitement.

After leaving her, Lady Theobald drove home to Oldclough Hall, rather out of humor. She had been rather out of humor for some time, having never quite recovered from her anger at the daring of that cheerful builder of mills, Mr. John Burmistone. Mr. Burmistone had been one innovation, and Octavia Bassett was another. She had not been able to manage Mr. Burmistone, and she was not at all sure that she had managed Octavia Bassett.

She entered the dining-room with an ominous frown on her forehead.

At the end of the table, opposite her own seat, was a vacant chair, and her frown deepened when she saw it.

"Where is Miss Gaston?" she demanded of the servant.

Before the man had time to reply, the door opened, and a girl came in hurriedly, with a somewhat frightened air.

"I beg pardon, grandmamma dear," she said, going to her seat quickly. "I did not know you had come home."

"We have a dinner-hour," announced her ladyship, "and *I* do not disregard it."

"I am very sorry," faltered the culprit.

"That is enough, Lucia," interrupted Lady Theobald; and Lucia dropped her eyes, and began to eat her soup with nervous haste. In fact, she was glad to escape so easily.

She was a very pretty creature, with brown eyes, a soft white skin, and a slight figure with a reed-like grace. A great quantity of brown hair was twisted into an ugly coil on the top of her delicate little head; and she wore an ugly muslin gown of Miss Chickie's make.

For some time the meal progressed in dead silence; but at length Lucia ventured to raise her eyes.

"I have been walking in Slowbridge, grandmamma," she said, "and I met Mr. Burmistone, who told me that Miss Bassett has a visitor — a young lady from America."

Lady Theobald laid her knife and fork down deliberately.

"Mr. Burmistone?" she said. "Did I understand you to say that you stopped on the roadside to converse with Mr. Burmistone?"

Lucia colored up to her delicate eyebrows and above them.

"I was trying to reach a flower growing on the bank," she said, "and he was so kind as to stop to get it for me. I did not know he was near at first. And then he inquired how you were — and told me he had just heard about the young lady."

"Naturally!" remarked her ladyship sardonically. "It is as I anticipated it would be. We shall find Mr. Burmistone at our elbows upon all occasions. And he will not allow himself to be easily driven away. He is as determined as persons of his class usually are."

"O grandmamma!" protested Lucia, with innocent fervor. "I really do not think he is — like that at all. I could not help thinking he was very gentlemanly and kind. He is so much interested in your school, and so anxious that it should prosper."

"May I ask," inquired Lady Theobald, "how long a time this generous expression of his sentiments occupied? Was this the reason of your forgetting the dinner-hour?"

"We did not" — said Lucia guiltily: "it did not take many minutes. I — I do not think that made me late."

Lady Theobald dismissed this paltry excuse with one remark, — a remark made in the deep tones referred to once before.

"I should scarcely have expected," she observed, "that a granddaughter of mine would have spent half an hour conversing on the public road with the proprietor of Slowbridge Mills."

"O grandmamma!" exclaimed Lucia, the tears rising in her eyes: "it was not half an hour."

"I should scarcely have expected," replied her ladyship, "that a granddaughter of mine would have spent five minutes conversing on the public road with the proprietor of Slowbridge Mills."

To this assault there seemed to be no reply to make. Lady Theobald had her granddaughter under excellent control. Under her rigorous rule, the girl — whose mother had died at her birth — had been brought up. At nineteen she was simple, sensitive, shy. She had been permitted to have no companions, and the greatest excitements of her life had been the Slowbridge tea-parties. Of the late Sir Gilbert Theobald, the less said the better. He had spent very little of his married life at Oldclough Hall, and upon his death his widow had found herself possessed of a substantial, gloomy mansion, an exalted position in Slowbridge society, and a small marriage-settlement, upon which she might make all the efforts she chose to sustain her state. So Lucia wore her dresses a much longer time than any other Slowbridge young lady: she was obliged to mend her little gloves again and again; and her hats were retrimmed so often that even Slowbridge thought them old-fashioned. But she was too simple and sweet-natured to be much troubled, and indeed thought very little about the matter. She was only troubled when Lady Theobald scolded her, which was by no means infrequently. Perhaps the straits to which, at times, her ladyship was put to maintain her dignity imbittered her somewhat.

"Lucia is neither a Theobald nor a Barold," she had been heard to say once, and she had said it with much rigor.

A subject of much conversation in private circles had been Lucia's future. It had been discussed in whispers since her seventeenth year, but no one had seemed to approach any solution of the difficulty. Upon the subject of her plans for her granddaughter, Lady Theobald had preserved stern silence. Once, and once only, she had allowed herself to be betrayed into the expression of a sentiment connected with the matter.

"If Miss Lucia marries"—a matron of reckless proclivities had remarked.

Lady Theobald turned upon her, slowly and majestically.

"*If* Miss Gaston marries," she repeated. "Does it seem likely that Miss Gaston will *not* marry?"

This settled the matter finally. Lucia was to be married when Lady Theobald thought fit. So far, however, she had not thought fit: indeed, there had been nobody for Lucia to marry,—nobody whom her grandmother would have allowed her to marry, at least. There were very few young men in Slowbridge; and the very few were scarcely eligible according to Lady Theobald's standard, and—if such a thing should be mentioned—to Lucia's, if she had known she had one, which she certainly did not.

CHAPTER VI.

ACCIDENTAL.

WHEN dinner was over, Lady Theobald rose, and proceeded to the drawing-room, Lucia following in her wake. From her very babyhood Lucia had disliked the drawing-room, which was an imposing apartment of great length and height, containing much massive furniture, upholstered in faded blue satin. All the girl's evenings, since her fifth year, had been spent sitting opposite her grandmother, in one of the straightest of the blue chairs: all the most scathing reproofs she had received had been administered to her at such times. She had a secret theory, indeed, that all unpleasant things occurred in the drawing-room after dinner.

Just as they had seated themselves, and Lady Theobald was on the point of drawing toward her the little basket containing the gray woollen mittens she made a duty of employing herself by knitting each evening, Dobson, the coachman, in his character of footman, threw open the door, and announced a visitor.

"Capt. Barold."

Lady Theobald dropped her gray mitten, the steel needles falling upon the table with a clink. She rose to her feet at once, and met half-way the young man who had entered.

"My dear Francis," she remarked, "I am exceedingly glad to see you at last," with a slight emphasis upon the "at last."

"Tha-anks," said Capt. Barold, rather languidly. "You're very good, I'm sure."

Then he glanced at Lucia, and Lady Theobald addressed her:—

"Lucia," she said, "this is Francis Barold, who is your cousin."

Capt. Barold shook hands feebly.

"I have been trying to find out whether it is third or fourth," he said.

"It is third," said my lady.

Lucia had never seen her display such cordiality to anybody. But Capt. Francis Barold did not seem much impressed by it. It struck Lucia that he would not be likely to be impressed by any thing. He seated himself near her grandmother's chair, and proceeded to explain his presence on the spot, without exhibiting much interest even in his own relation of facts.

"I promised the Rathburns that I would spend a week at their place; and Slowbridge was on the way, so it occurred to me I would drop off in passing. The Rathburns' place, Broadoaks, is about ten miles farther on; not far, you see."

"Then," said Lady Theobald, "I am to understand that your visit is accidental."

Capt. Barold was not embarrassed. He did not attempt to avoid her ladyship's rather stern eye, as he made his cool reply.

"Well, yes," he said. "I beg pardon, but it is accidental, rather."

Lucia gave him a pretty, frightened look, as if she felt that, after such an audacious confession, something very serious must happen; but nothing serious happened at all. Singularly enough, it was Lady Theobald herself who looked ill at ease, and as though she had not been prepared for such a contingency.

During the whole of the evening, in fact, it was always Lady Theobald who was placed at a disadvantage, Lucia discovered. She could hardly realize the fact at first; but before an hour had passed, its truth was forced upon her.

Capt. Barold was a very striking-looking man, upon the whole. He was large, gracefully built, and fair: his eyes were gray, and noticeable for the coldness of their expression, his features regular and aquiline, his movements leisurely.

As he conversed with her grandmother, Lucia wondered at him privately. It seemed to her innocent mind that he had been everywhere, and seen every thing and everybody, without caring for or enjoying his privileges. The truth was, that he had seen and experienced a great deal too much. As an only child, the heir to a large property, and heir prospective to one of the oldest titles in the country, he had exhausted life early. He saw in Lady Theobald, not the imposing head and social front of Slowbridge social life, the power who rewarded with approval and punished with a frown, but a tiresome, pretentious old woman, whom his mother had asked him, for some feminine reason, to visit.

"She feels she has a claim upon us, Francis," she had said appealingly.

"Well," he had remarked, "that is rather deuced cool, isn't it? We have people enough on our hands without cultivating Slowbridge, you know."

His mother sighed faintly.

"It is true we have a great many people to consider; but I wish you would do it, my dear."

She did not say any thing at all about Lucia: above all, she did not mention that a year ago she herself had spent two or three days at Slowbridge, and had been charmed beyond measure by the girl's innocent freshness, and that she had said, rather absently, to Lady Theobald, —

"What a charming wife Lucia would make for a man to whom gentleness and a yielding disposition were necessary! We do not find such girls in society nowadays, my dear Lady Theobald. It is very difficult of late years to find a girl who is not spoken of as 'fast,' and who is not disposed to take the reins in her own hands. Our young men are flattered and courted until they become a little dictatorial, and our girls are spoiled at home. And the result is a great deal of domestic unhappiness afterward — and even a great deal of scandal, which is dreadful to contemplate. I cannot help feeling the greatest anxiety in secret concerning Francis. Young men so seldom consider these matters until it is too late."

"Girls are not trained as they were in my young days, or even in yours," said Lady Theobald. "They are allowed too much liberty. Lucia has been brought up immediately under my own eye."

"I feel that it is fortunate," remarked Mrs. Barold, quite incidentally, "that Francis need not make a point of money."

For a few moments Lady Theobald did not respond; but afterward, in the course of the conversation which followed, she made an observation which was, of course, purely incidental.

"If Lucia makes a marriage which pleases her great-uncle, old Mr. Dugald Binnie, of

Glasgow, she will be a very fortunate girl. He has intimated, in his eccentric fashion, that his immense fortune will either be hers, or will be spent in building charitable asylums of various kinds. He is a remarkable and singular man."

When Capt. Barold had entered his distinguished relative's drawing-room, he had not regarded his third cousin with a very great deal of interest. He had seen too many beauties in his thirty years to be greatly moved by the sight of one; and here was only a girl who had soft eyes, and looked young for her age, and who wore an ugly muslin gown, that most girls could not have carried off at all.

"You have spent the greater part of your life in Slowbridge?" he condescended to say in the course of the evening.

"I have lived here always," Lucia answered. "I have never been away more than a week at a time."

"Ah?" interrogatively. "I hope you have not found it dull."

"No," smiling a little. "Not very. You see, I have known nothing gayer."

"There is society enough of a harmless kind here," spoke up Lady Theobald virtuously. "I do not approve of a round of gayeties for young people: it unfits them for the duties of life."

But Capt. Barold was not as favorably impressed by these remarks as might have been anticipated.

"What an old fool she is!" was his polite inward comment. And he resolved at once to make his visit as brief as possible, and not to be induced to run down again during his stay at Broadoaks. He did not even take the trouble to appear to enjoy his evening. From his earliest infancy, he had always found it easier to please himself than to please other people. In fact, the world had devoted itself to endeavoring to please him, and win his — toleration, we may say, instead of admiration, since it could not hope for the latter. At home he had been adored rapturously by a large circle of affectionate male and female relatives; at school his tutors had been singularly indulgent of his faults and admiring of his talents; even among his fellow-pupils he had been a sort of autocrat.

Why not, indeed, with such birthrights and such prospects? When he had entered society, he had met with even more amiable treatment from affectionate mothers, from innocent daughters, from cordial paternal parents, who voted him an exceedingly fine fellow. Why should he bore himself by taking the trouble to seem pleased by a stupid evening with an old grenadier in petticoats and a badly dressed country girl?

Lucia was very glad when, in answer to a timidly appealing glance, Lady Theobald said, —

"It is half-past ten. You may wish us good-night, Lucia."

Lucia obeyed, as if she had been half-past ten herself, instead of nearly twenty; and Barold was not long in following her example.

Dobson led him to a stately chamber at the top of the staircase, and left him there. The captain chose the largest and most luxurious chair, sat down in it, and lighted a cigar at his leisure.

"Confoundedly stupid hole!" he said with

a refined vigor one would scarcely have expected from an individual of his birth and breeding. "I shall leave to-morrow, of course. What was my mother thinking of? Stupid business from first to last."

CHAPTER VII.

"I SHOULD LIKE TO SEE MORE OF SLOWBRIDGE."

When he announced at breakfast his intention of taking his departure on the midday train, Lucia wondered again what would happen; and again, to her relief, Lady Theobald was astonishingly lenient.

"As your friends expect you, of course we cannot overrule them," she said. "We will, however, hope to see something of you during your stay at Broadoaks. It will be very easy for you to run down and give us a few hours now and then."

"Tha-anks," said Capt. Barold.

He was decently civil, if not enthusiastic, during the few remaining hours of his stay. He sauntered through the grounds with Lucia, who took charge of him in obedience to her grandmother's wish. He did not find her particularly troublesome when she was away from her ladyship's side. When she came out to him in her simple cotton gown and straw hat, it occurred to him that she was much prettier than he had thought her at first. For economical reasons she had made the little morning-dress herself, without the slightest regard for the designs of Miss Chickie; and as it was not trimmed at all, and had only a black-velvet ribbon at the waist, there was nothing to place her charming figure at a disadvantage. It could not be said that her shyness and simplicity delighted Capt. Barold, but, at least, they did not displease him; and this was really as much as could be expected.

"She does not expect a fellow to exert himself, at all events," was his inward comment; and he did not exert himself.

But, when on the point of taking his departure, he went so far as to make a very gracious remark to her.

"I hope we shall have the pleasure of seeing you in London for a season, before very long," he said: "my mother will have great pleasure in taking charge of you, if Lady Theobald cannot be induced to leave Slowbridge."

"Lucia never goes from home alone," said Lady Theobald; "but I should certainly be obliged to call upon your mother for her good offices, in the case of our spending a season in London. I am too old a woman to alter my mode of life altogether."

In obedience to her ladyship's orders, the venerable landau was brought to the door; and the two ladies drove to the station with him.

It was during this drive that a very curious incident occurred, — an incident to which, perhaps, this story owes its existence, since, if it had not taken place, there might, very possibly, have been no events of a stirring nature to chronicle. Just as Dobson drove rather slowly up the part of High Street distinguished by the presence of Miss Belinda Bassett's house, Capt. Barold suddenly appeared to be attracted by some figure he discovered in the garden appertaining to that modest structure.

"By Jove!" he exclaimed, in an undertone, "there is Miss Octavia."

For the moment he was almost roused to a display of interest. A faint smile lighted his face, and his cold, handsome eyes slightly brightened.

Lady Theobald sat bolt upright.

"That is Miss Bassett's niece, from America," she said. "Do I understand you know her?"

Capt. Barold turned to confront her, evidently annoyed at having allowed a surprise to get the better of him. All expression died out of his face.

"I travelled with her from Framwich to Stamford," he said. "I suppose we should have reached Slowbridge together, but that I dropped off at Stamford to get a newspaper, and the train left me behind."

"O grandmamma!" exclaimed Lucia, who had turned to look, "how very pretty she is!"

Miss Octavia certainly was amazingly so this morning. She was standing by a rose-bush again, and was dressed in a cashmere morning-robe of the finest texture and the faintest pink: it had a Watteau plait down the back, a *jabot* of lace down the front, and the close, high frills of lace around the throat which seemed to be a weakness with her.

Her hair was dressed high upon her head, and showed to advantage her little ears and as much of her slim white neck as the frills did not conceal.

But Lady Theobald did not share Lucia's enthusiasm.

"She looks like an actress," she said. "If the trees were painted canvas and the roses artificial, one might have some patience with her. That kind of thing is scarcely what we expect in Slowbridge."

Then she turned to Barold.

"I had the pleasure of meeting her yesterday, not long after she arrived," she said. "She had diamonds in her ears as big as peas, and rings to match. Her manner is just what one might expect from a young woman brought up among gold-diggers and silver-miners."

"It struck me as being a very unique and interesting manner," said Capt. Barold. "It is chiefly noticeable for a *sang-froid* which might be regarded as rather enviable. She was good enough to tell me all about her papa and the silver-mines, and I really found the conversation entertaining."

"It is scarcely customary for English young women to confide in their masculine travelling companions to such an extent," remarked my lady grimly.

"She did not confide in me at all," said Barold. "Therein lay her attraction. One cannot submit to being 'confided in' by a strange young woman, however charming. This young lady's remarks were flavored solely with an adorably cool candor. She evidently did not desire to appeal to any emotion whatever."

And as he leaned back in his seat, he still looked at the picturesque figure which they had passed, as if he would not have been sorry to see it turn its head toward him.

In fact, it seemed that, notwithstanding his usual good fortune, Capt. Barold was doomed this morning to make remarks of a nature objectionable to his revered relation. On their way they passed Mr. Burmistone's mill, which was at work in all its vigor, with a whir and buzz of machinery, and a slight odor of oil in its surrounding atmosphere.

"Ah!" said Mr. Barold, putting his single eyeglass into his eye, and scanning it after the manner of experts. "I did not think you had any thing of that sort here. Who put it up?"

"The man's name," replied Lady Theobald severely, "is Burmistone."

"Pretty good idea, isn't it?" remarked Barold. "Good for the place — and all that sort of thing."

"To my mind," answered my lady, "it is the worst possible thing which could have happened."

Mr. Francis Barold dropped his eyeglass dexterously, and at once lapsed into his normal condition — which was a condition by no means favorable to argument.

"Think so?" he said slowly. "Pity, isn't it, under the circumstances?"

And really there was nothing at all for her ladyship to do but preserve a lofty silence. She had scarcely recovered herself when they reached the station, and it was necessary to say farewell as complacently as possible.

"We will hope to see you again before many days," she said with dignity, if not with warmth.

Mr. Francis Barold was silent for a second,

and a slightly reflective expression flitted across his face.

"Thanks, yes," he said at last. "Certainly. It is easy to come down, and I should like to see more of Slowbridge."

When the train had puffed in and out of the station, and Dobson was driving down High Street again, her ladyship's feelings rather got the better of her.

"If Belinda Bassett is a wise woman," she remarked, "she will take my advice, and get rid of this young lady as soon as possible. It appears to me," she continued, with exalted piety, "that every well-trained English girl has reason to thank her Maker that she was born in a civilized land."

"Perhaps," suggested Lucia softly, "Miss Octavia Bassett has had no one to train her at all; and it may be that — that she even feels it deeply."

The feathers in her ladyship's bonnet trembled.

"She does not feel it at all!" she announced. "She is an impertinent — minx!"

CHAPTER VIII.

SHARES LOOKING UP.

THERE were others who echoed her ladyship's words afterward, though they echoed them privately, and with more caution than my lady felt necessary. It is certain that Miss Octavia Bassett did not improve as time progressed, and she had enlarged opportunities for studying the noble example set before her by Slowbridge.

On his arrival in New York, Martin Bassett telegraphed to his daughter and sister, per Atlantic cable, informing them that he might be detained a couple of months, and bidding them to be of good cheer. The arrival of the message in its official envelope so alarmed Miss Belinda, that she was supported by Mary Anne while it was read to her by Octavia, who received it without any surprise whatever. For some time after its completion, Slowbridge had privately disbelieved in the Atlantic cable, and, until this occasion, had certainly disbelieved in the existence of people who received messages through it. In fact, on first finding that she was the recipient of such a message, Miss Belinda had made immediate preparations for fainting quietly away, being fully convinced that a shipwreck had occurred, which had resulted in her brother's death, and that his executors had chosen this delicate method of breaking the news.

"A message by Atlantic cable?" she had gasped. "Don't — don't read it, my love. L-let some one else do that. Poor — poor child! Trust in Providence, my love, and — and bear up. Ah, how I wish I had a stronger mind, and could be of more service to you!"

"It's a message from father," said Octavia. "Nothing is the matter. He's all right. He got in on Saturday."

"Ah!" panted Miss Belinda. "Are you *quite* sure, my dear — are you quite sure?"

"That's what he says. Listen."

"Got in Saturday. Piper met me. Shares looking up. May be kept here two months. Will write. Keep up your spirits.

"MARTIN BASSETT."

"Thank Heaven!" sighed Miss Belinda. "Thank Heaven!"

"Why?" said Octavia.

"Why?" echoed Miss Belinda. "Ah, my dear, if you knew how terrified I was! I felt sure that something had happened. A *cable* message, my dear! I never received a telegram in my life before, and to receive a *cable* message was really a *shock*."

"Well, I don't see why," said Octavia. "It seems to me it is pretty much like any other message."

Miss Belinda regarded her timidly.

"Does your papa *often* send them?" she inquired. "Surely it must be expensive."

"I don't suppose it's cheap," Octavia replied, "but it saves time and worry. I should have had to wait twelve days for a letter."

"Very true," said Miss Belinda, "but" —

She broke off with rather a distressed shake of the head. Her simple ideas of economy and quiet living were frequently upset in these times. She had begun to regard her niece with a slight feeling of awe; and yet Octavia had not been doing any thing at all remarkable in her own eyes, and considered her life pretty dull.

If the elder Miss Bassett, her parents and grandparents, had not been so thoroughly well known, and so universally respected; if their social position had not been so firmly established, and their quiet lives not quite so highly respectable, — there is an awful possibility that Slowbridge might even have gone so far as not to ask Octavia out to tea at all. But even Lady Theobald felt that it would not do to slight Belinda Bassett's niece and guest. To omit the customary state teas would have been to crush innocent Miss Belinda at a blow, and place her — through the medium of this young lady, who alone deserved condemnation — beyond the pale of all social law.

"It is only to be regretted," said her ladyship, "that Belinda Bassett has not arranged things better. Relatives of such an order **are** certainly to be deplored."

In secret Lucia felt much soft-hearted sympathy for both Miss Bassett and her guest. She could not help wondering how Miss Belinda became responsible for the calamity which had fallen upon her. It really did not seem probable that she had been previously consulted as to the kind of niece she desired, or that she had, in a distinct manner, evinced a preference for a niece of this description.

"Perhaps, dear grandmamma," the girl ventured, "it is because Miss Octavia Bassett is so young that" —

"May I ask," inquired Lady Theobald, in fell tones, "how old you are?"

"I was nineteen in — in December."

"Miss Octavia Bassett," said her ladyship, "was nineteen last October, and it is now June. I have not yet found it necessary to apologize for you on the score of youth."

But it was her ladyship who took the initiative, and set an evening for entertaining Miss Belinda and her niece, in company with several other ladies, with the best bohea, thin bread and butter, plum-cake, and various other delicacies.

"What do they do at such places?" asked Octavia. "Half-past five is pretty early."

"We spend some time at the tea-table, my dear," explained Miss Belinda. "And afterward we — we converse. A few of us play whist. I do not. I feel as if I were not clever enough, and I get flurried too easily by — by differences of opinion."

"I should think it wasn't very exciting," said Octavia. "I don't fancy I ever went to an entertainment where they did nothing but drink tea, and talk."

"It is not our intention or desire to be exciting, my dear," Miss Belinda replied with mild dignity. "And an improving conversation is frequently most beneficial to the parties engaged in it."

"I'm afraid," Octavia observed, "that I never heard much improving conversation."

She was really no fonder of masculine society than the generality of girls; but she could not help wondering if there would be any young men present, and if, indeed, there were any young men in Slowbridge who might possibly be produced upon festive occasions, even though ordinarily kept in the background. She had not heard Miss Belinda mention any masculine name so far, but that of the curate of St. James's; and, when she had seen him pass the house, she had not found his slim, black figure, and faint, ecclesiastic whiskers, especially interesting.

It must be confessed that Miss Belinda suffered many pangs of anxiety in looking forward to her young kinswoman's first appearance in society. A tea at Lady Theobald's house constituted formal presentation to the Slowbridge world. Each young lady within the pale of genteel society, having arrived at years of discretion, on returning home from boarding-school, was invited to tea at Oldclough Hall. During an entire evening she was the subject of watchful criticism. Her deportment was remarked, her accomplishments displayed, she performed her last new "pieces" upon the piano, she was drawn into conversation by her hostess; and upon the timid modesty of her replies, and the reverence of her listening attitudes, depended her future social status. So it was very natural indeed that Miss Belinda should be anxious.

"I would wear something rather quiet and — and simple, my dear Octavia," she said. "A white muslin perhaps, with blue ribbons."

"Would you?" answered Octavia. Then, after appearing to reflect upon the matter a few seconds, "I've got one that would do, if it's warm enough to wear it. I bought it in New York, but it came from Paris. I've never worn it yet."

"It would be nicer than any thing else, my love," said Miss Belinda, delighted to find her difficulty so easily disposed of. "Nothing is so charming in the dress of a young girl as pure simplicity. Our Slowbridge young ladies rarely wear any thing but white for evening. Miss Chickie assured me, a few weeks ago, that she had made fifteen white-muslin dresses, all after one simple design of her own."

"I shouldn't think that was particularly nice, myself," remarked Octavia impartially. "I should be glad one of the fifteen didn't belong to me. I should feel as if people might say, when I came into a room, 'Good gracious, there's another!'"

"The first was made for Miss Lucia Gaston, who is Lady Theobald's niece," replied Miss Belinda mildly. "And there are few young ladies in Slowbridge who would not emulate her example."

"Oh!" said Octavia, "I dare say she is very nice, and all that; but I don't believe I should care to copy her dresses. I think I should draw the line there."

But she said it without any ill-nature; and, sensitive as Miss Belinda was upon the subject of her cherished ideals, she could not take offence.

When the eventful evening arrived, there was excitement in more than one establishment upon High Street and the streets in its vicinity. The stories of the diamonds, the gold-diggers, and the silver-mines, had been added to, and embellished, in the most ornate and startling manner. It was well known that only Lady Theobald's fine appreciation of Miss Belinda Bassett's feelings had induced her to extend her hospitalities to that lady's niece.

"I would prefer, my dear," said more than one discreet matron to her daughter, as they attired themselves, — "I would much prefer that you would remain near me during the earlier part of the evening, before we know how this young lady may turn out. Let your manner toward her be kind, but not familiar. It is well to be upon the safe side."

What precise line of conduct it was generally anticipated that this gold-digging and silver-mining young person would adopt, it would be difficult to say: it is sufficient that the general sentiments regarding her were of a distrustful, if not timorous, nature.

To Miss Bassett, who felt all this in the very air she breathed, the girl's innocence of the condition of affairs was even a little touching. With all her splendor, she was not at all hard to please, and had quite awakened to an interest in the impending social event. She seemed in good spirits, and talked more than was her custom, giving Miss Belinda graphic descriptions of various festal gatherings she had attended in New York, when she seemed to have been very gay indeed, and to have worn very beautiful dresses, and also to have had rather more than her share of partners. The phrases she used, and the dances she described, were all strange to Miss Belinda, and tended to reducing her to a bewildered condition, in which she felt much timid amazement at the intrepidity of the New-York young ladies, and no slight suspicion of the "German" — as a theatrical kind of dance, involving extraordinary figures, and an extraordinary amount of attention from partners of the stronger sex.

It must be admitted, however, that by this time, notwithstanding the various shocks she had received, Miss Belinda had begun to discover in her young guest divers good qualities which appealed to her affectionate and susceptible old heart. In the first place, the girl had no small affectations: indeed, if she had been less unaffected she might have been less subject to severe comment. She was good-natured, and generous to extravagance. Her manner toward Mary Anne never ceased to arouse Miss Belinda to interest. There was not any condescension whatever in it, and yet it could not be called a vulgarly familiar manner: it was rather an astonishingly simple manner, somehow suggestive of a subtile recognition of Mary Anne's youth, and ill-luck in not having before her more lively prospects. She gave Mary Anne presents in the shape of articles of clothing at which Slowbridge would have exclaimed in horror if the recipient had dared to wear them; but, when Miss Belinda expressed her regret at these indiscretions, Octavia was quite willing to rectify her mistakes.

"Ah, well!" she said, "I can give her some money, and she can buy some things for herself." Which she proceeded to do; and when, under her mistress's direction, Mary Anne purchased a stout brown merino, she took quite an interest in her struggles at making it.

"I wouldn't make it so short in the waist and so full in the skirt, if I were you," she said. "There's no reason why it shouldn't fit, you know," thereby winning the housemaiden's undying adoration, and adding much to the shapeliness of the garment.

"I am sure she has a good heart," Miss Belinda said to herself, as the days went by. "She is like Martin in that. I dare say she finds me very ignorant and silly. I often see in her face that she is unable to understand my feeling about things; but she never seems to laugh at me, nor think of me unkindly. And she is very, very pretty, though perhaps I ought not to think of that at all."

CHAPTER IX.

WHITE MUSLIN.

As the good little spinster was arraying herself on this particular evening, having laid upon the bed the greater portion of her modest splendor, she went to her wardrobe, and took therefrom the sacred bandbox containing her best cap. All the ladies of Slowbridge wore caps; and all being respectfully plagiarized from Lady Theobald, without any reference to age, size, complexion, or demeanor, the result was sometimes a little trying. Lady Theobald's head-dresses were of a severe and bristling order. The lace of which they were composed was induced by some ingenious device to form itself into aggressive quillings, the bows seemed lined with buckram, the strings neither floated nor fluttered.

"To a majestic person the style is very

appropriate," Miss Belinda had said to Octavia that very day; "but to one who is not so, it is rather trying. Sometimes, indeed, I have *almost* wished that Miss Chickie would vary a *little* more in her designs."

Perhaps the sight of the various articles contained in two of the five trunks had inspired these doubts in the dear old lady's breast: it is certain, at least, that, as she took the best cap up, a faint sigh fluttered upon her lips.

"It is very large for a small person," she said. "And I am not at all sure that amber is becoming to me."

And just at that moment there came a tap at the door, which she knew was from Octavia.

She laid the cap back, in some confusion at being surprised in a moment of weakness.

"Come in, my love," she said.

Octavia pushed the door open, and came in. She had not dressed yet, and had on her wrapper and slippers, which were both of quilted gray silk, gayly embroidered with carnations. But Miss Belinda had seen both wrapper and slippers before, and had become used to their sumptuousness: what she had not seen was the trifle the girl held in her hand.

"See here," she said. "See what I have been making for you!"

She looked quite elated, and laughed triumphantly.

"I did not know I could do it until I tried," she said. "I had seen some in New York, and I had the lace by me. And I have enough left to make ruffles for your neck and wrists. It's Mechlin."

"My dear!" exclaimed Miss Belinda. "My dear!"

Octavia laughed again.

"Don't you know what it is?" she said. "It isn't like a Slowbridge cap; but it's a cap, nevertheless. They wear them like this in New York, and I think they are ever so much prettier."

It was true that it was not like a Slowbridge cap, and was also true that it was prettier. It was a delicate affair of softly quilled lace, adorned here and there with loops of pale satin ribbon.

"Let me try it on," said Octavia, advancing; and in a minute she had done so, and turned Miss Bassett about to face herself in the glass. "There!" she said. "Isn't that better than — well, than emulating Lady Theobald?"

It was so pretty and so becoming, and Miss Belinda was so touched by the girl's innocent enjoyment, that the tears came into her eyes.

"My — my love," she faltered, "it is so beautiful, and so expensive, that — though indeed I don't know how to thank you — I am afraid I should not dare to wear it."

"Oh!" answered Octavia, "that's nonsense, you know. I'm sure there's no reason why people shouldn't wear becoming things. Besides, I should be awfully disappointed. I didn't think I could make it, and I'm real proud of it. You don't know how becoming it is!"

Miss Belinda looked at her reflection, and faltered. It was becoming.

"My love," she protested faintly, "real Mechlin! There is really no such lace in Slowbridge."

"All the better," said Octavia cheerfully.

"I'm glad to hear that. It isn't one bit too nice for you."

To Miss Belinda's astonishment, she drew a step nearer to her, and gave one of the satin loops a queer, caressing little touch, which actually seemed to mean something. And then suddenly the girl stooped, with a little laugh, and gave her aunt a light kiss on her cheek.

"There!" she said. "You must take it from me for a present. I'll go and make the ruffles this minute; and you must wear those too, and let people see how stylish you can be."

And, without giving Miss Bassett time to speak, she ran out of the room, and left the dear old lady warmed to the heart, tearful, delighted, frightened.

A coach from the Blue Lion had been ordered to present itself at a quarter past five, promptly; and at the time specified it rattled up to the door with much spirit, — with so much spirit, indeed, that Miss Belinda was a little alarmed.

"Dear, dear!" she said. "I hope the driver will be able to control the horse, and will not allow him to go too fast. One hears of such terrible accidents."

Then Mary Anne was sent to announce the arrival of the equipage to Miss Octavia, and, having performed the errand, came back beaming with smiles.

"Oh, mum," she exclaimed, "you never see nothin' like her! Her gownd is 'evingly. An' lor'! how you do look yourself, to be sure!"

Indeed, the lace ruffles on her "best" black silk, and the little cap on her smooth hair, had done a great deal for Miss Bassett; and she had only just been reproaching herself for her vanity in recognizing this fact. But Mary Anne's words awakened a new train of thought.

"Is — is Miss Octavia's dress a showy one, Mary Anne?" she inquired. "Dear me, I do hope it is not a showy dress!"

"I never see nothin' no eleganter, mum," said Mary Anne: "she wants nothin' but a veil to make a bride out of her — an' a becominer thing she never has wore."

They heard the soft sweep of skirts at that moment, and Octavia came in.

"There!" she said, stopping when she had reached the middle of the room. "Is that simple enough?"

Miss Belinda could only look at her helplessly. The "white muslin" was composed almost entirely of Valenciennes lace; the blue ribbons were embroidered with field-daisies; the air of delicate elaborateness about the whole was something which her innocent mind could not have believed possible in orthodox white and blue.

"I don't think I should call it exactly simple," she said. "My love, what a quantity of lace!"

Octavia glanced down at her *jabots* and frills complacently.

"There *is* a good deal of it," she remarked; "but then, it is nice, and one can stand a good deal of nice Valenciennes on white. They said Worth made the dress. I hope he did. It cost enough. The ribbon was embroidered by hand, I suppose. And there is plenty of it cut up into these bows."

There was no more to be said. Miss Belinda led the way to the coach, which they entered under the admiring or critical eyes of several most respectable families, who had been lying in wait behind their window-curtains since they had been summoned there by the sound of the wheels.

As the vehicle rattled past the boarding-school, all the young ladies in the first class rushed to the window. They were rewarded for their zeal by a glimpse of a cloud of muslin and lace, a charmingly dressed yellow-brown head, and a pretty face, whose eyes favored them with a frank stare of interest.

"She had diamonds in her ears!" cried Miss Phipps, wildly excited. "I saw them flash. Ah, how I should like to see her without her wraps! I have no doubt she is a perfect blaze!"

CHAPTER X.

ANNOUNCING MR. BAROLD.

LADY THEOBALD'S invited guests sat in the faded blue drawing-room, waiting. Everybody had been unusually prompt, perhaps because everybody wished to be on the ground in time to see Miss Octavia Bassett make her entrance.

"I should think it would be rather a trial, even to such a girl as she is said to be," remarked one matron.

"It is but natural that she should feel that Lady Theobald will regard her rather critically, and that she should know that American manners will hardly be the thing for a genteel and conservative English country town."

"We saw her a few days ago," said Lucia, who chanced to hear this speech, "and she is very pretty. I think I never saw any one so very pretty before."

"But in quite a theatrical way, I think, my dear," the matron replied, in a tone of gentle correction.

"I have seen so very few theatrical people," Lucia answered sweetly, "that I scarcely know what the theatrical way is, dear Mrs. Burnham. Her dress was very beautiful, and not like what we wear in Slowbridge; but she seemed to me to be very bright and pretty, in a way quite new to me, and so just a little odd."

"I have heard that her dress is most extravagant and wasteful," put in Miss Pilcher, whose educational position entitled her to the condescending respect of her patronesses. "She has lace on her morning gowns, which"—

"Miss Bassett and Miss Octavia Bassett," announced Dobson, throwing open the door.

Lady Theobald rose from her seat. A slight rustle made itself heard through the company, as the ladies all turned toward the entrance; and, after they had so turned, there were evidences of a positive thrill. Before the eyes of all, Belinda Bassett advanced with rich ruffles of Mechlin at her neck and wrists, with a delicate and distinctly novel cap upon her head, her niece following her with an unabashed face, twenty pounds' worth of lace on her dress, and unmistakable diamonds in her little ears.

"There is not a *shadow* of timidity about her," cried Mrs. Burnham under her breath. "This is actual boldness."

But this was a very severe term to use, notwithstanding that it was born of righteous indignation. It was not boldness at all: it was only the serenity of a young person who was quite unconscious that there was any thing to fear in the rather unimposing party before her. Octavia was accustomed to entering rooms full of strangers. She had spent several years of her life in hotels, where she had been stared out of countenance by a few score new people every day. She was even used to being, in some sort, a young person of note. It was nothing unusual for her to know that she was being pointed out. "That pretty blonde," she often heard it said, "is Martin Bassett's daughter: sharp fellow, Bassett,—and lucky fellow too; more money than he can count."

ANNOUNCING MR. BAROLD. 93

So she was not at all frightened when she walked in behind Miss Belinda. She glanced about her cheerfully, and, catching sight of Lucia, smiled at her as she advanced up the room. The call of state Lady Theobald had made with her grand-daughter had been a very brief one; but Octavia had taken a decided fancy to Lucia, and was glad to see her again.

"I am glad to see you, Belinda," said her ladyship, shaking hands. "And you also, Miss Octavia."

"Thank you," responded Octavia.

"You are very kind," Miss Belinda murmured gratefully.

"I hope you are both well?" said Lady Theobald with majestic condescension, and in tones to be heard all over the room.

"Quite well, thank you," murmured Miss Belinda again. "*Very* well indeed;" rather as if this fortunate state of affairs was the result of her ladyship's kind intervention with the fates.

She felt terribly conscious of being the centre of observation, and rather overpowered by the novelty of her attire, which was plainly creating a sensation. Octavia, however, who was far more looked at, was entirely oblivious of the painful prominence of her position. She remained standing in the middle of the room, talking to Lucia, who had approached to greet her. She was so much taller than Lucia, that she looked very tall indeed by contrast, and also very wonderfully dressed. Lucia's white muslin was one of Miss Chickie's fifteen, and was, in a "genteel" way, very suggestive of Slowbridge. Suspended from Octavia's waist by a long loop of the embroidered ribbon, was a little round fan, of downy pale-blue feathers, and with this she played as she talked; but Lucia, having nothing to play with, could only stand with her little hands hanging at her sides.

"I have never been to an afternoon tea like this before," Octavia said. "It is nothing like a kettle-drum."

"I am not sure that I know what a kettle-drum is," Lucia answered. "They have them in London, I think; but I have never been to London."

"They have them in New York," said

Octavia; "and they are a crowded sort of afternoon parties, where ladies go in carriage-toilet, not evening dress. People are rushing in and out all the time."

Lucia glanced around the room and smiled.

"That is very unlike this," she remarked.

"Well," said Octavia, "I should think that, after all, this might be nicer."

Which was very civil.

Lucia glanced around again — this time rather stealthily — at Lady Theobald. Then she glanced back at Octavia.

"But it isn't," she said, in an undertone.

Octavia began to laugh. They were on a new and familiar footing from that moment.

"I said 'it might,'" she answered.

She was not afraid, any longer, of finding the evening stupid. If there were no young men, there was at least a young woman who was in sympathy with her. She said, —

"I hope that I shall behave myself pretty well, and do the things I am expected to do."

"Oh!" said Lucia, with a rather alarmed expression, "I hope so. I — I am afraid you would not be comfortable if you didn't."

Octavia opened her eyes, as she often did

at Miss Belinda's remarks, and then suddenly she began to laugh again.

"What would they do?" she said disrespectfully. "Would they turn me out, without giving me any tea?"

Lucia looked still more frightened.

"Don't let them see you laughing," she said. "They — they will say you are giddy."

"Giddy!" replied Octavia. "I don't think there is any thing to make me giddy here."

"If they say you are giddy," said Lucia, "your fate will be sealed; and, if you are to stay here, it really will be better to try to please them a little."

Octavia reflected a moment.

"I don't mean to *dis*please them," she said, "unless they are very easily displeased. I suppose I don't think very much about what people are saying of me. I don't seem to notice."

"Will you come now and let me introduce Miss Egerton and her sister?" suggested Lucia hurriedly. "Grandmamma is looking at us."

In the innocence of her heart Octavia

glanced at Lady Theobald, and saw that she was looking at them, and with a disapproving air.

"I wonder what that's for?" she said to herself; but she followed Lucia across the room.

She made the acquaintance of the Misses Egerton, who seemed rather fluttered, and, after the first exchange of civilities, subsided into monosyllables and attentive stares. They were, indeed, very anxious to hear Octavia converse, but had not the courage to attempt to draw her out, unless a sudden query of Miss Lydia's could be considered such an attempt.

"Do you like England?" she asked.

"Is this England?" inquired Octavia.

"It is a part of England, of course," replied the young lady, with calm literalness.

"Then, of course, I like it very much," said Octavia, slightly waving her fan and smiling.

Miss Lydia Egerton and Miss Violet Egerton each regarded her in dubious silence for a moment. They did not think she looked as if she were "clever;" but the speech sounded to both as if she were, and as if she meant to be clever a little at their expense.

Naturally, after that they felt slightly uncomfortable, and said less than before; and conversation lagged to such an extent that Octavia was not sorry when tea was announced.

And it so happened that tea was not the only thing announced. The ladies had all just risen from their seats with a gentle rustle, and Lady Theobald was moving forward to marshal her procession into the dining-room, when Dobson appeared at the door again.

"Mr. Barold, my lady," he said, "and Mr. Burmistone."

Everybody glanced first at the door, and then at Lady Theobald. Mr. Francis Barold crossed the threshold, followed by the tall, square-shouldered builder of mills, who was a strong, handsome man, and bore himself very well, not seeming to mind at all the numerous eyes fixed upon him.

"I did not know," said Barold, "that we should find you had guests. Beg pardon, I'm sure, and so does Burmistone, whom I had the pleasure of meeting at Broadoaks, and who was good enough to invite me to return with him."

Lady Theobald extended her hand to the gentleman specified.

"I am glad," she said rigidly, "to see Mr. Burmistone."

Then she turned to Barold.

"This is very fortunate," she announced. "We are just going in to take tea, in which I hope you will join us. Lucia"—

Mr. Francis Barold naturally turned, as her ladyship uttered her granddaughter's name in a tone of command. It may be supposed that his first intention in turning was to look at Lucia; but he had scarcely done so, when his attention was attracted by the figure nearest to her,—the figure of a young lady, who was playing with a little blue fan, and smiling at him brilliantly and unmistakably.

The next moment he was standing at Octavia Bassett's side, looking rather pleased, and the blood of Slowbridge was congealing, as the significance of the situation was realized.

One instant of breathless — of awful — suspense, and her ladyship recovered herself.

"We will go in to tea," she said. "May I ask you, Mr. Burmistone, to accompany Miss Pilcher?"

CHAPTER XI.

A SLIGHT INDISCRETION.

During the remainder of the evening, Miss Belinda was a prey to wretchedness and despair. When she raised her eyes to her hostess, she met with a glance full of icy significance; when she looked across the tea-table, she saw Octavia seated next to Mr. Francis Barold, monopolizing his attention, and apparently in the very best possible spirits. It only made matters worse, that Mr. Francis Barold seemed to find her remarks worthy of his attention. He drank very little tea, and now and then appeared much interested and amused. In fact, he found Miss Octavia even more entertaining than he had found her during their journey. She did not hesitate at all to tell him that she was delighted to see him again at this particular juncture.

"You don't know how glad I was to see you come in," she said.

She met his rather startled glance with the most open candor as she spoke.

"It is very civil of you to say so," he said; "but you can hardly expect me to believe it, you know. It is too good to be true."

"I thought it was too good to be true when the door opened," she answered cheerfully. "I should have been glad to see *anybody*, almost"—

"Well, that," he interposed, "isn't quite so civil."

"It is not quite so civil to"—

But there she checked herself, and asked him a question with the most *naïve* seriousness.

"Are you a great friend of Lady Theobald's?" she said.

"No," he answered. "I am a relative."

"That's worse," she remarked.

"It is," he replied. "Very much worse."

"I asked you," she proceeded, with an entrancing little smile of irreverent approval, "because I was going to say that my last speech was not quite so civil to Lady Theobald."

"That is perfectly true," he responded. "It wasn't civil to her at all."

He was passing his time very comfortably, and was really surprised to feel that he was more interested in these simple audacities than he had been in any conversation for some time. Perhaps it was because his companion was so wonderfully pretty, but it is not unlikely that there were also other reasons. She looked him straight in the eyes, she comported herself after the manner of a young lady who was enjoying herself, and yet he felt vaguely that she might have enjoyed herself quite as much with Burmistone, and that it was probable that she would not think a second time of him, or of what she said to him.

After tea, when they returned to the drawing-room, the opportunities afforded for conversation were not numerous. The piano was opened, and one after another of the young ladies were invited to exhibit their prowess. Upon its musical education Slowbridge prided itself. "Few towns," Miss Pilcher frequently remarked, "could be congratulated upon the possession of *such* talent and *such* cultivation." The Misses Egerton played a duet, the Misses Loftus sang, Miss Abercrombie "executed" a sonata with such effect as to melt Miss Pilcher to tears; and still Octavia had not been called upon. There might have been a reason for this, or there might not; but the moment arrived, at length, when Lady Theobald moved toward Miss Belinda with evidently fell intent.

"Perhaps," she said, "perhaps your niece, Miss Octavia, will favor us."

Miss Belinda replied in a deprecatory and uncertain murmur.

"I — am not sure. I really don't know. Perhaps — Octavia, my dear."

Octavia raised a smiling face.

"I don't play," she said. "I never learned."

"You do not play!" exclaimed Lady Theobald. "You do not play at all!"

"No," answered Octavia. "Not a note. And I think I am rather glad of it; because, if I tried, I should be sure to do it worse than other people. I would rather," with unimpaired cheerfulness, "let some one else do it."

There were a few seconds of dead silence.

A dozen people seated around her had heard. Miss Pilcher shuddered; Miss Belinda looked down; Mr. Francis Barold preserved an entirely unmoved countenance, the general impression being that he was very much shocked, and concealed his disgust with an effort.

"My dear," said Lady Theobald, with an air of much condescension and some grave pity, "I should advise you to try to learn. I can assure you that you would find it a great source of pleasure."

"If you could assure me that my friends would find it a great source of pleasure, I might begin," answered the mistaken young person, still cheerfully; "but I am afraid they wouldn't."

It seemed that fate had marked her for disgrace. In half an hour from that time she capped the climax of her indiscretions.

The evening being warm, the French windows had been left open; and, in passing one of them, she stopped a moment to look out at the brightly moonlit grounds.

Barold, who was with her, paused too.

"Looks rather nice, doesn't it?" he said.

"Yes," she replied. "Suppose we go out on the terrace."

He laughed in an amused fashion she did not understand.

"Suppose we do," he said. "By Jove, that's a good idea!"

He laughed as he followed her.

"What amuses you so?" she inquired.

"Oh!" he replied, "I am merely thinking of Lady Theobald."

"Well, she commented, "I think it's rather disrespectful in you to laugh. Isn't it a lovely night? I didn't think you had such moonlight nights in England. What a night for a drive!"

"Is that one of the things you do in America — drive by moonlight?"

"Yes. Do you mean to say you don't do it in England?"

"Not often. Is it young ladies who drive by moonlight in America?"

"Well, you don't suppose they go alone, do you?" quite ironically. "Of course they have some one with them."

"Ah! Their papas?"

"No."

"Their mammas?"

"No."

"Their governesses, their uncles, their aunts?"

"No," with a little smile.

He smiled also.

"That is another good idea," he said. "You have a great many nice ideas in America."

She was silent a moment or so, swinging her fan slowly to and fro by its ribbon, and appearing to reflect.

"Does that mean," she said at length, "that it wouldn't be considered proper in England?"

"I hope you won't hold me responsible for English fallacies," was his sole answer.

"I don't hold anybody responsible for them," she returned with some spirit. "I don't care one thing about them."

"That is fortunate," he commented. "I am happy to say I don't, either. I take the liberty of pleasing myself. I find it pays best."

"Perhaps," she said, returning to the charge, "perhaps Lady Theobald will think *this* is improper."

He put his hand up, and stroked his mustache lightly, without replying.

"But it is *not*," she added emphatically: "it is *not!*"

"No," he admitted, with a touch of irony, "it is not!"

"Are *you* any the worse for it?" she demanded.

"Well, really, I think not — as yet," he replied.

"Then we won't go in," she said, the smile returning to her lips again.

CHAPTER XII.

AN INVITATION.

In the mean time Mr. Burmistone was improving his opportunities within doors. He had listened to the music with the most serious attention; and on its conclusion he had turned to Mrs. Burnham, and made himself very agreeable indeed. At length, however, he arose, and sauntered across the room to a table at which Lucia Gaston chanced to be standing alone, having just been deserted by a young lady whose mamma had summoned her. She wore, Mr. Burmistone regretted to see, as he advanced, a troubled and anxious expression; the truth being that she had a moment before remarked the exit of Miss Belinda's niece and her companion. It happened oddly that Mr. Burmistone's first words touched upon the subject of her thought. He began quite abruptly with it.

"It seems to me," he said, "that Miss Octavia Bassett"—

Lucia stopped him with a courage which surprised herself.

"Oh, if you please," she implored, "don't say any thing unkind about her!"

Mr. Burmistone looked down into her soft eyes with a good deal of feeling.

"I was not going to say any thing unkind," he answered. "Why should I?"

"Everybody seems to find a reason for speaking severely of her," Lucia faltered. "I have heard so many unkind things to-night, that I am quite unhappy. I am sure — I am *sure* she is very candid and simple."

"Yes," answered Mr. Burmistone, "I am sure she is very candid and simple."

"Why should we expect her to be exactly like ourselves?" Lucia went on. "How can we be sure that our way is better than any other? Why should they be angry because her dress is so expensive and pretty? Indeed, I only wish I had such a dress. It is a thousand times prettier than any we ever wear. Look around the room, and see if it is not. And as to her not having learned to play on the piano, or to speak French — why should she be obliged to do things she feels she would not be clever at? I am not clever, and have been a sort of slave all my life, and have been scolded and blamed for what I could not help at all, until I have felt as if I must be a criminal. How happy she must have been to be let alone!"

She had clasped her little hands, and, though she spoke in a low voice, was quite impassioned in an unconscious way. Her brief girlish life had not been a very happy one, as may be easily imagined; and a glimpse of the liberty for which she had suffered roused her to a sense of her own wrongs.

"We are all cut out after the same pattern," she said. "We learn the same things, and wear the same dresses, one might say. What Lydia Egerton has been taught, I have been taught; yet what two creatures could be more unlike each other, by nature, than we are?"

Mr. Burmistone glanced across the room at Miss Egerton. She was a fine, robust young woman, with a high nose and a stolid expression of countenance.

"That is true," he remarked.

"We are afraid of every thing," said Lucia bitterly. "Lydia Egerton is afraid — though you might not think so. And, as for me, nobody knows what a coward I am but myself. Yes, I am a coward! When grandmamma looks at me, I tremble. I dare not speak my mind, and differ with her, when I know she is unjust and in the wrong. No one could say that of Miss Octavia Bassett."

"That is perfectly true," said Mr. Burmistone; and he even went so far as to laugh as he thought of Miss Octavia trembling in the august presence of Lady Theobald.

The laugh checked Lucia at once in her little outburst of eloquence. She began to blush, the color mounting to her forehead.

"Oh!" she began, "I did not mean to — to say so much. I "—

There was something so innocent and touching in her sudden timidity and confusion, that Mr. Burmistone forgot altogether that they were not very old friends, and that Lady Theobald might be looking.

He bent slightly forward, and looked into her upraised, alarmed eyes.

AN INVITATION.

"Don't be afraid of *me*," he said; "don't, for pity's sake!"

He could not have hit upon a luckier speech, and also he could not have uttered it more feelingly than he did. It helped her to recover herself, and gave her courage.

"There," she said, with a slight catch of the breath, "does not that prove what I said to be true? I was afraid, the very moment I ceased to forget myself. I was afraid of you and of myself. I have no courage at all."

"You will gain it in time," he said.

"I shall try to gain it," she answered. "I am nearly twenty, and it is time that I should learn to respect myself. I think it must be because I have no self-respect that I am such a coward."

It seemed that her resolution was to be tried immediately; for at that very moment Lady Theobald turned, and, on recognizing the full significance of Lucia's position, was apparently struck temporarily dumb and motionless. When she recovered from the shock, she made a majestic gesture of command.

Mr. Burmistone glanced at the girl's face, and saw that it changed color a little. "Lady Theobald appears to wish to speak to you," he said.

Lucia left her seat, and walked across the room with a steady air. Lady Theobald did not remove her eye from her until she stopped within three feet of her. Then she asked a rather unnecessary question: —

"With whom have you been conversing?"

"With Mr. Burmistone."

"Upon what subject?"

"We were speaking of Miss Octavia Bassett."

Her ladyship glanced around the room, as if a new idea had occurred to her, and said, —

"Where *is* Miss Octavia Bassett?"

Here it must be confessed that Lucia faltered.

"She is on the terrace with Mr. Barold."

"She is on"—

Her ladyship stopped short in the middle of her sentence. This was too much for her. She left Lucia, and crossed the room to Miss Belinda.

"Belinda," she said, in an awful under-

AN INVITATION. 115

tone, "your niece is out upon the terrace with Mr. Barold. Perhaps it would be as well for you to intimate to her that in England it is not customary — that — Belinda, go and bring her in."

Miss Belinda arose, actually looking pale. She had been making such strenuous efforts to converse with Miss Pilcher and Mrs. Burnham, that she had been betrayed into forgetting her charge. She could scarcely believe her ears. She went to the open window, and looked out, and then turned paler than before.

"Octavia, my dear," she said faintly.

"Francis!" said Lady Theobald, over her shoulder.

Mr. Francis Barold turned a rather bored countenance toward them; but it was evidently not Octavia who had bored him.

"Octavia," said Miss Belinda, "how imprudent! In that thin dress — the night air! How could you, my dear, how could you?"

"Oh! I shall not catch cold," Octavia answered. "I am used to it. I have been out hours and hours, on moonlight nights, at home."

But she moved toward them.

"You must remember," said Lady Theobald, "that there are many things which may be done in America which would not be safe in England."

And she made the remark in an almost sepulchral tone of warning.

How Miss Belinda would have supported herself if the coach had not been announced at this juncture, it would be difficult to say. The coach was announced, and they took their departure. Mr. Barold happening to make his adieus at the same time, they were escorted by him down to the vehicle from the Blue Lion.

When he had assisted them in, and closed the door, Octavia bent forward, so that the moonlight fell full on her pretty, lace-covered head, and the sparkling drops in her ears.

"Oh!" she exclaimed, "if you stay here at all, you must come and see us. — Aunt Belinda, ask him to come and see us."

Miss Belinda could scarcely speak.

"I shall be most — most happy," she fluttered. "Any — friend of dear Lady Theobald's, of course" —

AN INVITATION.

"Don't forget," said Octavia, waving her hand.

The coach moved off, and Miss Belinda sank back into a dark corner.

"My dear," she gasped, "what will he think?"

Octavia was winding her lace scarf around her throat.

"He'll think I want him to call," she said serenely. "And I do."

CHAPTER XIII.

INTENTIONS.

THE position in which Lady Theobald found herself placed, after these occurrences, was certainly a difficult and unpleasant one. It was Mr. Francis Barold's caprice, for the time being, to develop an intimacy with Mr. Burmistone. He had, it seemed, chosen to become interested in him during their sojourn at Broadoaks. He had discovered him to be a desirable companion, and a clever, amiable fellow. This much he condescended to explain incidentally to her ladyship's self.

"I can't say I expected to meet a nice fellow or a companionable fellow," he remarked, "and I was agreeably surprised to find him both. Never says too much or too little. Never bores a man."

To this Lady Theobald could make no reply. Singularly enough, she had discovered early in their acquaintance that her wonted weapons were likely to dull their edges upon the steely coldness of Mr. Francis Barold's impassibility. In the presence of this fortunate young man, before whom his world had bowed the knee from his tenderest infancy, she lost the majesty of her demeanor. He refused to be affected by it: he was even implacable enough to show openly that it bored him, and to insinuate by his manner that he did not intend to submit to it. He entirely ignored the claim of relationship, and acted according to the promptings of his own moods. He did not feel it at all incumbent upon him to remain at Oldclough Hall, and subject himself to the time-honored customs there in vogue. He preferred to accept Mr. Burmistone's invitation to become his guest at the handsome house he had just completed, in which he lived in bachelor splendor. Accordingly he installed himself there, and thereby complicated matters greatly.

Slowbridge found itself in a position as difficult as, and far more delicate than, Lady Theobald's. The tea-drinkings in honor of that troublesome young person, Miss Octavia

Bassett, having been inaugurated by her ladyship, must go the social rounds, according to ancient custom. But what, in discretion's name, was to be done concerning Mr. Francis Barold? There was no doubt whatever that he must not be ignored; and, in that case, what difficulties presented themselves!

The mamma of the two Misses Egerton, who was a nervous and easily subjugated person, was so excited and overwrought by the prospect before her, that, in contemplating it when she wrote her invitations, she was affected to tears.

"I can assure you, Lydia," she said, "that I have not slept for three nights, I have been so harassed. Here, on one hand, is Mr. Francis Barold, who must be invited; and on the other is Mr. Burmistone, whom we cannot pass over; and here is Lady Theobald, who will turn to stone the moment she sees him,—though, goodness knows, I am sure he seems a very quiet, respectable man, and said some of the most complimentary things about your playing. And here is that dreadful girl, who is enough to give one cold chills, and who may do all sorts of dreadful things, and is certainly a living example to all respectable, well-educated girls. And the blindest of the blind could see that nothing would offend Lady Theobald more fatally than to let her be thrown with Francis Barold; and how one is to invite them into the same room, and keep them apart, I'm sure I don't know how. Lady Theobald herself could not do it, and how can we be expected to? And the refreshments on my mind too; and Forbes failing on her tea-cakes, and bringing up Sally Lunns like lead."

That these misgivings were equally shared by each entertainer in prospective, might be adduced from the fact that the same afternoon Mrs. Burnham and Miss Pilcher appeared upon the scene, to consult with Mrs. Egerton upon the subject.

Miss Lydia and Miss Violet being dismissed up-stairs to their practising, the three ladies sat in the darkened parlor, and talked the matter over in solemn conclave.

"I have consulted Miss Pilcher, and mentioned the affair to Mrs. Gibson," announced Mrs. Burnham. "And, really, we have not yet been able to arrive at any conclusion."

Mrs. Egerton shook her head tearfully.

"Pray don't come to me, my dears," she said, — "don't, I beg of you! I have thought about it until my circulation has all gone wrong, and Lydia has been applying hot-water bottles to my feet all the morning. I gave it up at half-past two, and set Violet to writing invitations to one and all, let the consequences be what they may."

Miss Pilcher glanced at Mrs. Burnham, and Mrs. Burnham glanced at Miss Pilcher.

"Perhaps," Miss Pilcher suggested to her companion, "it would be as well for you to mention your impressions."

Mrs. Burnham's manner became additionally cautious. She bent forward slightly.

"My dear," she said, "has it struck you that Lady Theobald has any — intentions, so to speak?"

"Intentions?" repeated Mrs. Egerton.

"Yes," with deep significance, — "so to speak. With regard to Lucia."

Mrs. Egerton looked utterly helpless.

"Dear me!" she ejaculated plaintively. "I have never had time to think of it. Dear me! With regard to Lucia!"

Mrs. Burnham became more significant still.

"*And*," she added, "Mr. Francis Barold."

Mrs. Egerton turned to Miss Pilcher, and saw confirmation of the fact in her countenance.

"Dear, dear!" she said. "That makes it worse than ever."

"It is certain," put in Miss Pilcher, "that the union would be a desirable one; and we have reason to remark that a deep interest in Mr. Francis Barold has been shown by Lady Theobald. He has been invited to make her house his home during his stay in Slowbridge; and, though he has not done so, the fact that he has not is due only to some inexplicable reluctance upon his own part. And we all remember that Lady Theobald once plainly intimated that she anticipated Lucia forming, in the future, a matrimonial alliance."

"Oh!" commented Mrs. Egerton, with some slight impatience, "it is all very well for Lady Theobald to have intentions for Lucia; but, if the young man has none, I really don't see that her intentions will be likely to result in any thing particular. And I am sure Mr. Francis Barold is not in the mood to be influenced in that way now. He is more likely to entertain himself with Miss Octavia Bassett, who will take him out in the moonlight, and make herself agreeable to him in her American style."

Miss Pilcher and Mrs. Burnham exchanged glances again.

"My dear," said Mrs. Burnham, "he has called upon her twice since Lady Theobald's tea. They say she invites him herself, and flirts with him openly in the garden."

"Her conduct is such," said Miss Pilcher, with a shudder, "that the blinds upon the side of the seminary which faces Miss Bassett's garden are kept closed by my orders. I have young ladies under my care whose characters are in process of formation, and whose parents repose confidence in me."

"Nothing but my friendship for Belinda Bassett," remarked Mrs Burnham, "would induce me to invite the girl to my house." Then she turned to Mrs. Egerton. "But — ahem — have you included them *all* in your invitations?" she observed.

Mrs. Egerton became plaintive again.

"I don't see how I could be expected to do any thing else," she said. "Lady Theobald herself could not invite Mr. Francis Barold from Mr. Burmistone's house, and leave Mr. Burmistone at home. And, after all, I must say it is my opinion nobody would have objected to Mr. Burmistone, in the first place, if Lady Theobald had not insisted upon it."

Mrs. Burnham reflected.

"Perhaps that is true," she admitted cautiously at length. "And it must be confessed that a man in his position is not entirely without his advantages — particularly in a place where there are but few gentlemen, and those scarcely desirable as " —

She paused there discreetly, but Mrs. Egerton was not so discreet.

"There are a great many young ladies in Slowbridge," she said, shaking her head, — "a great many! And with five in a family, all old enough to be out of school, I am sure it is flying in the face of Providence to neglect one's opportunities."

When the two ladies took their departure, Mrs. Burnham seemed reflective. Finally she said, —

"Poor Mrs. Egerton's mind is not what it was, and it never was remarkably strong. It must be admitted, too, that there is a lack of — of delicacy. Those great plain girls of hers must be a trial to her."

As she spoke they were passing the privet hedge which surrounded Miss Bassett's house and garden; and a sound caused both to glance around. The front door had just been opened; and a gentleman was descending the steps, — a young gentleman in neat clerical garb, his guileless ecclesiastical countenance suffused with mantling blushes of confusion and delight. He stopped on the gravel path to receive the last words of Miss Octavia Bassett, who stood on the threshold, smiling down upon him in the prettiest way in the world.

"Tuesday afternoon," she said. "Now don't forget; because I shall ask Mr. Barold and Miss Gaston, on purpose to play against us. Even St. James can't object to croquet."

"I — indeed, I shall be *most* happy and

— and delighted," stammered her departing guest, " if you will be so kind as to — to instruct me, and forgive my awkwardness."

"Oh! I'll instruct you," said Octavia. " I have instructed people before, and I know how."

Mrs. Burnham clutched Miss Pilcher's arm.

" Do you see who *that* is? " she demanded. " Would you have believed it? "

Miss Pilcher preserved a stony demeanor.

" I would believe any thing of Miss Octavia Bassett," she replied. " There would be nothing at all remarkable, to my mind, in her flirting with the bishop himself! Why should she hesitate to endeavor to entangle the curate of St. James? "

CHAPTER XIV.

A CLERICAL VISIT.

It was indeed true that the Rev. Arthur Poppleton had spent the greater part of his afternoon in Miss Belinda Bassett's front parlor, and that Octavia had entertained him in such a manner that he had been beguiled into forgetting the clerical visits he had intended to make, and had finally committed himself by a promise to return a day or two later to play croquet. His object in calling had been to request Miss Belinda's assistance in a parochial matter. His natural timorousness of nature had indeed led him to put off making the visit for as long a time as possible. The reports he had heard of Miss Octavia Bassett had inspired him with great dread. Consequently he had presented himself at Miss Belinda's front door with secret anguish.

"Will you say," he had faltered to Mary

Anne, "that it is Mr. Poppleton, to see *Miss* Bassett — Miss *Belinda* Bassett?"

And then he had been handed into the parlor, the door had been closed behind him, and he had found himself shut up entirely alone in the room with Miss Octavia Bassett herself.

His first impulse was to turn, and flee precipitately: indeed, he even went so far as to turn, and clutch the handle of the door; but somehow a second thought arrived in time to lead him to control himself.

This second thought came with his second glance at Octavia.

She was not at all what he had pictured her. Singularly enough, no one had told him that she was pretty; and he had thought of her as a gaunt young person, with a determined and manly air. She struck him, on the contrary, as being extremely girlish and charming to look upon. She wore the pale pink gown; and as he entered he saw her give a furtive little dab to her eyes with a lace handkerchief, and hurriedly crush an open letter into her pocket. Then, seeming to dismiss her emotion with enviable facility, she rose to greet him.

"If you want to see aunt Belinda," she said, "perhaps you had better sit down. She will be here directly."

He plucked up spirit to take a seat, suddenly feeling his terror take wing. He was amazed at his own courage.

"Th-thank you," he said. "I have the pleasure of" — There, it is true, he stopped, looked at her, blushed, and finished somewhat disjointedly. "Miss Octavia Bassett, I believe."

"Yes," she answered, and sat down near him.

When Miss Belinda descended the stairs, a short time afterward, her ears were greeted by the sound of brisk conversation, in which the Rev. Arthur Poppleton appeared to be taking part with before-unheard-of spirit. When he arose at her entrance, there was in his manner an air of mild buoyancy which astonished her beyond measure. When he re-seated himself, he seemed quite to forget the object of his visit for some minutes, and was thus placed in the embarrassing position of having to refer to his note-book.

Having done so, and found that he had

called to ask assistance for the family of one of his parishioners, he recovered himself somewhat. As he explained the exigencies of the case, Octavia listened.

"Well," she said, "I should think it would make you quite uncomfortable, if you see things like that often."

"I regret to say I do see such things only too frequently," he answered.

"Gracious!" she said; but that was all.

He was conscious of being slightly disappointed at her apathy; and perhaps it is to be deplored that he forgot it afterward, when Miss Belinda had bestowed her mite, and the case was dismissed for the time being. He really did forget it, and was beguiled into making a very long call, and enjoying himself as he had never enjoyed himself before.

When, at length, he was recalled to a sense of duty by a glance at the clock, he had already before his eyes an opening vista of delights, taking the form of future calls, and games of croquet played upon Miss Belinda's neatly-shaven grass-plat. He had bidden the ladies adieu in the parlor, and, having stepped into the hall, was fumbling rather excitedly in the umbrella-stand for his own especially slender clerical umbrella, when he was awakened to new rapture by hearing Miss Octavia's tone again.

He turned, and saw her standing quite near him, looking at him with rather an odd expression, and holding something in her hand.

"Oh!" she said. "See here, — those people."

"I — beg pardon," he hesitated. "I don't quite understand."

"Oh, yes!" she answered. "Those desperately poor wretches, you know, with fever, and leaks in their house, and all sorts of disagreeable things the matter with them. Give them this, won't you?"

"This" was a pretty silk purse, through whose meshes he saw the gleam of gold coin.

"That?" he said. "You don't mean — isn't there a good deal — I beg pardon — but really" —

"Well, if they are as poor as you say they are, it won't be too much," she replied. "I don't suppose they'll object to it: do you?"

She extended it to him as if she rather wished to get it out of her hands.

"You'd better take it," she said. "I shall spend it on something I don't need, if you don't. I'm always spending money on things I don't care for afterward."

He was filled with remorse, remembering that he had thought her apathetic.

"I — I really thought you were not interested at all," he burst forth. "Pray forgive me. This is generous indeed."

She looked down at some particularly brilliant rings on her hand, instead of looking at him.

"Oh, well!" she said, "I think it must be simply horrid to have to do without things. I can't see how people live. Besides, I haven't denied myself any thing. It would be worth talking about if I had, I suppose. Oh! by the by, never mind telling any one, will you?"

Then, without giving him time to reply, she raised her eyes to his face, and plunged into the subject of the croquet again, pursuing it until the final moment of his exit and departure, which was when Mrs. Burnham and Miss Pilcher had been scandalized at the easy freedom of her adieus.

CHAPTER XV.

SUPERIOR ADVANTAGES.

When Mr. Francis Barold called to pay his respects to Lady Theobald, after partaking of her hospitality, Mr. Burmistone accompanied him; and, upon almost every other occasion of his presenting himself to her ladyship, Mr. Burmistone was his companion.

It may as well be explained at the outset, that the mill-owner of Burmistone Mills was a man of decided determination of character, and that, upon the evening of Lady Theobald's tea, he had arrived at the conclusion that he would spare no effort to gain a certain end he felt it would add to his happiness to accomplish.

"I stand rather in awe of Lady Theobald, as any ordinary man would," he had said dryly to Barold, on their return to his house. "But my awe of her is not so great yet that I shall allow it to interfere with any of my plans."

"Have you any especial plan?" inquired Barold carelessly, after a pause.

"Yes," answered Mr. Burmistone, — "several. I should like to go to Oldclough rather often."

"I feel it the civil thing to go to Oldclough oftener than I like. Go with me."

"I should like to be included in all the invitations to tea for the next six months."

"I shall be included in all the invitations so long as I remain here; and it is not likely you will be left out in the cold. After you have gone the rounds once, you won't be dropped."

"Upon the whole, it appears so," said Mr. Burmistone. "Thanks."

So, at each of the tea-parties following Lady Theobald's, the two men appeared together. The small end of the wedge being inserted into the social stratum, the rest was not so difficult. Mrs. Burnham was at once surprised and overjoyed by her discoveries of the many excellences of the man they had so hastily determined to ignore. Mrs. Abercrombie found Mr. Burmistone's manner all that could be desired. Miss Pilcher expressed the highest appreciation of his views upon feminine education and "our duty to the young in our charge." Indeed, after Mrs. Egerton's evening, the tide of public opinion turned suddenly in his favor.

Public opinion did not change, however, as far as Octavia was concerned. Having had her anxiety set at rest by several encouraging paternal letters from Nevada, she began to make up her mind to enjoy herself, and was, it is to be regretted, betrayed by her youthful high spirits into the committing of numerous indiscretions. Upon each festal occasion she appeared in a new and elaborate costume: she accepted the attentions of Mr. Francis Barold, as if it were the most natural thing in the world that they should be offered; she joked — in what Mrs. Burnham designated "her Nevada way" — with the Rev. Arthur Poppleton, who appeared more frequently than had been his habit at the high teas. She played croquet with that gentleman and Mr. Barold day after day, upon the grass-plat, before all the eyes gazing down upon her from the neighboring windows; she managed to coerce Mr. Burmistone into joining these innocent orgies; and, in fact, to quote Miss Pilcher, there was "no limit to the shamelessness of her unfeminine conduct."

Several times much comment had been aroused by the fact that Lucia Gaston had been observed to form one of the party of players. She had indeed played with Barold, against Octavia and Mr. Poppleton, on the memorable day upon which that gentleman had taken his first lesson.

Barold had availed himself of the invitation extended to him by Octavia, upon several occasions, greatly to Miss Belinda's embarrassment. He had dropped in the evening after the curate's first call.

"Is Lady Theobald very fond of you?" Octavia had asked, in the course of this visit.

"It is very kind of her, if she is," he replied with languid irony.

"Isn't she fond enough of you to do any thing you ask her?" Octavia inquired.

"Really, I think not," he replied. "Imagine the degree of affection it requires! I am not fond enough of any one to do any thing they ask me."

Octavia bestowed a long look upon him.

"Well," she remarked, after a pause, "I believe you are not. I shouldn't think so."

Barold colored very faintly.

"I say," he said, "is that an imputation, or something of that character? It sounds like it, you know."

Octavia did not reply directly. She laughed a little.

"I want you to ask Lady Theobald to do something," she said.

"I am afraid I am not in such favor as you imagine," he said, looking slightly annoyed.

"Well, I think she won't refuse you this thing," she went on. "If she didn't loathe me so, I would ask her myself."

He deigned to smile.

"Does she loathe you?" he inquired.

"Yes," nodding. "She would not speak to me if it weren't for aunt Belinda. She thinks I am fast and loud. Do *you* think I am fast and loud?"

He was taken aback, and not for the first

time, either. She had startled and discomposed him several times in the course of their brief acquaintance; and he always resented it, priding himself in private, as he did, upon his coolness and immobility. He could not think of the right thing to say just now, so he was silent for a second.

"Tell me the truth," she persisted. "I shall not care — much."

"I do not think you would care at all."

"Well, perhaps I shouldn't. Go on. Do you think I am fast?"

"I am happy to say I do not find you slow."

She fixed her eyes on him, smiling faintly.

"That means I am fast," she said. "Well, no matter. Will you ask Lady Theobald what I want you to ask her?"

"I should not say you were fast at all," he said rather stiffly. "You have not been educated as — as Lady Theobald has educated Miss Gaston, for instance."

"I should rather think not," she replied. Then she added, very deliberately, "She has had what you might call very superior advantages, I suppose."

Her expression was totally incomprehensible to him. She spoke with the utmost seriousness, and looked down at the table.

"That is derision, I suppose," he remarked restively.

She glanced up again.

"At all events," she said, "there is nothing to laugh at in Lucia Gaston. Will you ask Lady Theobald? I want you to ask her to let Lucia Gaston come and play croquet with us on Tuesday. She is to play with you against Mr. Poppleton and me."

"Who is Mr. Poppleton?" he asked, with some reserve. He did not exactly fancy sharing his entertainment with any ordinary outsider. After all, there was no knowing what this little American might do.

"He is the curate of the church," she replied, undisturbed. "He is very nice, and little, and neat, and blushes all over to the toes of his boots. He came to see aunt Belinda, and I asked him to come and be taught to play."

"Who is to teach him?"

"I am. I have taught at least twenty men in New York and San Francisco."

SUPERIOR ADVANTAGES. 141

"I hope he appreciates your kindness."

"I mean to try if I can make him forget to be frightened," she said, with a gay laugh.

It was certainly nettling to find his air of reserve and displeasure met with such inconsequent lightness. She never seemed to recognize the subtle changes of temperature expressed in his manner. Only his sense of what was due to himself prevented his being very chilly indeed; but as she went on with her gay chat, in utter ignorance of his mood, and indulged in some very pretty airy nonsense, he soon recovered himself, and almost forgot his private grievance.

Before going away, he promised to ask Lady Theobald's indulgence in the matter of Lucia's joining them in their game. One speech of Octavia's, connected with the subject, he had thought very pretty, as well as kind.

"I like Miss Gaston," she said. "I think we might be friends if Lady Theobald would let us. Her superior advantages might do me good. They might improve me," she went on, with a little laugh, "and I suppose

I need improving very much. All my advantages have been of one kind."

When he had left her, she startled Miss Belinda by saying,—

"I have been asking Mr. Barold if he thought I was fast; and I believe he does — in fact, I am sure he does."

"Ah, my dear, my dear!" ejaculated Miss Belinda, "what a terrible thing to say to a gentleman! What will he think?"

Octavia smiled one of her calmest smiles.

"Isn't it queer how often you say that!" she remarked. "I think I should perish if I had to pull myself up that way as you do. I just go right on, and never worry. I don't mean to do any thing queer, and I don't see why any one should think I do."

CHAPTER XVI.

CROQUET.

Lucia was permitted to form one of the players in the game of croquet, being escorted to and from the scene by Francis Barold. Perhaps it occurred to Lady Theobald that the contrast of English reserve and maidenliness with the free-and-easy manners of young women from Nevada might lead to some good result.

"I trust your conduct will be such as to show that you at least have resided in a civilized land," she said. "The men of the present day may permit themselves to be amused by young persons whose demeanor might bring a blush to the cheek of a woman of forty, but it is not their habit to regard them with serious intentions."

Lucia reddened. She did not speak, though she wished very much for the courage to utter the words which rose to her lips. Lately she had found that now and then, at times when she was roused to anger, speeches of quite a clever and sarcastic nature presented themselves to her mind. She was never equal to uttering them aloud; but she felt that in time she might, because of course it was quite an advance in spirit to think them, and face, even in imagination, the probability of astounding and striking Lady Theobald dumb with their audacity.

"It ought to make me behave very well," she was saying now to herself, "to have before me the alternative of not being regarded with serious intentions. I wonder if it is Mr. Poppleton or Francis Barold who might not regard me seriously. And I wonder if they are any coarser in America than we can be in England when we try."

She enjoyed the afternoon very much, particularly the latter part of it, when Mr. Burmistone, who was passing, came in, being invited by Octavia across the privet hedge. Having paid his respects to Miss Belinda, who sat playing propriety under a laburnum-tree, Mr. Burmistone crossed the grass-plat

CROQUET.   145

to Lucia herself. She was awaiting her "turn," and laughing at the ardent enthusiasm of Mr. Poppleton, who, under Octavia's direction, was devoting all his energies to the game: her eyes were bright, and she had lost, for the time being, her timid air of feeling herself somehow in the wrong.

"I am glad to see you here," said Mr. Burmistone.

"I am glad to be here," she answered. "It has been such a happy afternoon. Every thing has seemed so bright and — and different!"

"'Different' is a very good word," he said, laughing.

"It isn't a very bad one," she returned, "and it expresses a good deal."

"It does indeed," he commented.

"Look at Mr. Poppleton and Octavia," she began.

"Have you got to 'Octavia'?" he inquired.

She looked down and blushed.

"I shall not say 'Octavia' to grandmamma."

Then suddenly she glanced up at him.

"That is sly, isn't it?" she said. "Sometimes I think I am very sly, though I am sure it is not my nature to be so. I would rather be open and candid."

"It would be better," he remarked.

"You think so?" she asked eagerly.

He could not help smiling.

"Do you ever tell untruths to Lady Theobald?" he inquired. "If you do, I shall begin to be alarmed."

"I act them," she said, blushing more deeply. "I really do — paltry sorts of untruths, you know; pretending to agree with her when I don't; pretending to like things a little when I hate them. I have been trying to improve myself lately, and once or twice it has made her very angry. She says I am disobedient and disrespectful. She asked me, one day, if it was my intention to emulate Miss Octavia Bassett. That was when I said I could not help feeling that I had wasted time in practising."

She sighed softly as she ended.

In the mean time Octavia had Mr. Poppleton and Mr. Francis Barold upon her hands, and was endeavoring to do her duty as hostess by both of them. If it had been her intention to captivate these gentlemen, she could not have complained that Mr. Poppleton was wary or difficult game. His first fears allayed, his downward path was smooth, and rapid in proportion. When he had taken his departure with the little silk purse in his keeping, he had carried under his clerical vest a warmed and thrilled heart. It was a heart which, it must be confessed, was of the most inexperienced and susceptible nature. A little man of affectionate and gentle disposition, he had been given from his earliest youth to indulging in timid dreams of mild future bliss, — of bliss represented by some lovely being whose ideals were similar to his own, and who preferred the wealth of a true affection to the glitter of the giddy throng. Upon one or two occasions, he had even worshipped from afar; but as on each of these occasions his hopes had been nipped in the bud by the union of their object with some hollow worldling, his dream had, so far, never attained very serious proportions. Since he had taken up his abode in Slowbridge, he had felt himself a little overpowered by circumstances. It had been a source of painful embarrassment to him, to find his innocent presence capable of producing confusion in the breasts of young ladies who were certainly not more guileless than himself. He had been conscious that the Misses Egerton did not continue their conversation with freedom when he chanced to approach the group they graced; and he had observed the same thing in their companions, — an additional circumspection of demeanor, so to speak, a touch of new decorum, whose object seemed to be to protect them from any appearance of imprudence.

"It is almost as if they were afraid of me," he had said to himself once or twice. "Dear me! I hope there is nothing in my appearance to lead them to" —

He was so much alarmed by this dreadful thought, that he had ever afterward approached any of these young ladies with a fear and trembling which had not added either to his comfort or their own; consequently his path had not been a very smooth one.

"I respect the young ladies of Slowbridge," he remarked to Octavia that very afternoon. "There are some very remarkable young ladies here, — very remarkable indeed. They are interested in the church, and the poor, and the schools, and, indeed, in every thing, which is most unselfish and amiable. Young ladies have usually so much to distract their attention from such matters."

"If I stay long enough in Slowbridge," said Octavia, "I shall be interested in the church, and the poor, and the schools."

It seemed to the curate that there had never been any thing so delightful in the world as her laugh and her unusual remarks. She seemed to him so beautiful, and so exhilarating, that he forgot all else but his admiration for her. He enjoyed himself so much this afternoon, that he was almost brilliant, and excited the sarcastic comment of Mr. Francis Barold, who was not enjoying himself at all.

"Confound it!" said that gentleman to himself, as he looked on. "What did I come here for? This style of thing is just what I might have expected. She is amusing herself with that poor little cad now, and I am left in the cold. I suppose that is her habit with the young men in Nevada."

He had no intention of entering the lists with the Rev. Arthur Poppleton, or of concealing the fact that he felt that this little Nevada flirt was making a blunder. The sooner she knew it, the better for herself; so he played his game as badly as possible, and with much dignity.

But Octavia was so deeply interested in Mr. Poppleton's ardent efforts to do credit to her teaching, that she was apparently unconscious of all else. She played with great cleverness, and carried her partner to the terminus, with an eager enjoyment of her skill quite pleasant to behold. She made little darts here and there, advised, directed, and controlled his movements, and was quite dramatic in a small way when he made a failure.

Mrs. Burnham, who was superintending the proceeding, seated in her own easy-chair behind her window-curtains, was roused to virtuous indignation by her energy.

"There is no repose whatever in her manner," she said. "No dignity. Is a game of croquet a matter of deep moment? It seems to me that it is almost impious to devote one's mind so wholly to a mere means of recreation."

"She seems to be enjoying it, mamma," said Miss Laura Burnham, with a faint sigh. Miss Laura had been looking on over her parent's shoulder. "They all seem to be enjoying it. See how Lucia Gaston and Mr. Burmistone are laughing. I never saw Lucia look like that before. The only one who seems a little dull is Mr. Barold."

"He is probably disgusted by a freedom of manner to which he is not accustomed," replied Mrs. Burnham. "The only wonder is that he has not been disgusted by it before."

CHAPTER XVII.

ADVANTAGES.

The game over, Octavia deserted her partner. She walked lightly, and with the air of a victor, to where Barold was standing. She was smiling, and slightly flushed, and for a moment or so stood fanning herself with a gay Japanese fan.

"Don't you think I am a good teacher?" she asked at length.

"I should say so," replied Barold, without enthusiasm. "I am afraid I am not a judge."

She waved her fan airily.

"I had a good pupil," she said. Then she held her fan still for a moment, and turned fully toward him. "I have done something you don't like," she said. "I knew I had."

Mr. Francis Barold retired within himself at once. In his present mood it really appeared that she was assuming that he was very much interested indeed.

ADVANTAGES.

"I should scarcely take the liberty upon a limited acquaintance," he began.

She looked at him steadily, fanning herself with slow, regular movements.

"Yes," she remarked. "You're mad. I knew you were."

He was so evidently disgusted by this observation, that she caught at the meaning of his look, and laughed a little.

"Ah!" she said, "that's an American word, ain't it? It sounds queer to you. You say 'vexed' instead of 'mad.' Well, then, you are vexed."

"If I have been so clumsy as to appear ill-humored," he said, "I beg pardon. Certainly I have no right to exhibit such unusual interest in your conduct."

He felt that this was rather decidedly to the point, but she did not seem overpowered at all. She smiled anew.

"Anybody has a right to be mad — I mean vexed," she observed. "I should like to know how people would live if they hadn't. I am mad — I mean vexed — twenty times a day."

"Indeed?" was his sole reply.

"Well," she said, "I think it's real mean in you to be so cool about it when you remember what I told you the other day."

"I regret to say I don't remember just now. I hope it was nothing very serious."

To his astonishment she looked down at her fan, and spoke in a slightly lowered voice: —

"I told you that I wanted to be improved."

It must be confessed that he was mollified. There was a softness in her manner which amazed him. He was at once embarrassed and delighted. But, at the same time, it would not do to commit himself to too great a seriousness.

"Oh!" he answered, "that was a rather good joke, I thought."

"No, it wasn't," she said, perhaps even half a tone lower. "I was in earnest."

Then she raised her eyes.

"If you told me when I did any thing wrong, I think it might be a good thing," she said.

He felt that this was quite possible, and was also struck with the idea that he might find the task of mentor — so long as he remained entirely non-committal — rather interesting. Still, he could not afford to descend at once from the elevated stand he had taken.

"I am afraid you would find it rather tiresome," he remarked.

"I am afraid *you* would," she answered. "You would have to tell me of things so often."

"Do you mean seriously to tell me that you would take my advice?" he inquired.

"I mightn't take all of it," was her reply; "but I should take some — perhaps a great deal."

"Thanks," he remarked. "I scarcely think I should give you a great deal."

She simply smiled.

"I have never had any advice at all," she said. "I don't know that I should have taken it if I had — just as likely as not I shouldn't; but I have never had any. Father spoiled me. He gave me all my own way. He said he didn't care, so long as I had a good time; and I must say I have generally had a good time. I don't see how I could help it — with all my own way, and no one to worry. I wasn't sick, and I could buy any thing I liked, and all that: so I had a good time. I've read of girls, in books, wishing they had mothers to take care of them. I don't know that I ever wished for one particularly. I can take care of myself. I must say, too, that I don't think some mothers are much of an institution. I know girls who have them, and they are always worrying."

He laughed in spite of himself; and though she had been speaking with the utmost seriousness and *naïveté*, she joined him.

When they ceased, she returned suddenly to the charge.

"Now tell me what I have done this afternoon that isn't right," she said, — "that Lucia Gaston wouldn't have done, for instance. I say that, because I shouldn't mind being a little like Lucia Gaston — in some things."

"Lucia ought to feel gratified," he commented.

"She does," she answered. "We had a little talk about it, and she was as pleased

ADVANTAGES. 157

as could be. I didn't think of it in that way until I saw her begin to blush. Guess what she said."

"I am afraid I can't."

"She said she saw so many things to envy in me, that she could scarcely believe I wanted to be at all like her."

"It was a very civil speech," said Barold ironically. "I scarcely thought Lady Theobald had trained her so well."

"She meant it," said Octavia. "You mayn't believe it, but she did. I know when people mean things, and when they don't."

"I wish I did," said Barold.

Octavia turned her attention to her fan.

"Well, I am waiting," she said.

"Waiting?" he repeated.

"To be told of my faults."

"But I scarcely see of what importance my opinion can be."

"It is of some importance to me — just now."

The last two words rendered him really impatient, and, it may be, spurred him up.

"If we are to take Lucia Gaston as a

model," he said, "Lucia Gaston would possibly not have been so complaisant in her demeanor toward our clerical friend."

"Complaisant!" she exclaimed, opening her lovely eyes. "When I was actually plunging about the garden, trying to teach him to play. Well, I shouldn't call that being complaisant."

"Lucia Gaston," he replied, "would not say that she had been 'plunging' about the garden."

She gave herself a moment for reflection.

"That's true," she remarked, when it was over: "she wouldn't. When I compare myself with the Slowbridge girls, I begin to think I must say some pretty awful things."

Barold made no reply, which caused her to laugh a little again.

"You daren't tell me," she said. "Now, do I? Well, I don't think I want to know very particularly. What Lady Theobald thinks will last quite a good while. Complaisant!"

"I am sorry you object to the word," he said.

"Oh, I don't!" she answered. "I like it.

It sounds so much more polite than to say I was flirting and being fast."

"Were you flirting?" he inquired coldly.

He objected to her ready serenity very much.

She looked a little puzzled.

"You are very like aunt Belinda," she said.

He drew himself up. He did not think there was any point of resemblance at all between Miss Belinda and himself.

She went on, without observing his movement.

"You think every thing means something, or is of some importance. You said that just as aunt Belinda says, 'What will they think?' It never occurs to me that they'll think at all. Gracious! Why should they?"

"You will find they do," he said.

"Well," she said, glancing at the group gathered under the laburnum-tree, "just now aunt Belinda thinks we had better go over to her; so, suppose we do it? At any rate, I found out that I was too complaisant to Mr. Poppleton."

When the party separated for the afternoon, Barold took Lucia home, and Mr. Burmistone and the curate walked down the street together.

Mr. Poppleton was indeed most agreeably exhilarated. His expressive little countenance beamed with delight.

"What a very charming person Miss Bassett is!" he exclaimed, after they had left the gate. "What a very charming person indeed!"

"Very charming," said Mr. Burmistone with much seriousness. "A prettier young person I certainly have never seen; and those wonderful gowns of hers"—

"Oh!" interrupted Mr. Poppleton, with natural confusion, "I — referred to Miss Belinda Bassett; though, really, what you say is very true. Miss Octavia Bassett — indeed — I think — in fact, Miss Octavia Bassett is *quite*, one might almost say even *more*, charming than her aunt."

"Yes," admitted Mr. Burmistone; "perhaps one might. She is less ripe, it is true; but that is an objection time will remove."

"There is such a delightful gayety in her manner!" said Mr. Poppleton; "such an ingenuous frankness! such a — a — such spirit! It quite carries me away with it, — quite."

He walked a few steps, thinking over this delightful gayety and ingenuous frankness; and then burst out afresh, —

"And what a remarkable life she has had too! She actually told me, that, once in her childhood, she lived for months in a gold-diggers' camp, — the only woman there She says the men were kind to her, and made a pet of her. She has known the most extraordinary people."

In the mean time Francis Barold returned Lucia to Lady Theobald's safe keeping. Having done so, he made his adieus, and left the two to themselves. Her ladyship was, it must be confessed, a little at a loss to explain to herself what she saw, or fancied she saw, in the manner and appearance of her young relative. She was persuaded that she had never seen Lucia look as she looked this afternoon. She had a brighter color in her cheeks than usual, her pretty figure seemed more erect, her eyes had a spirit in them which was quite new. She had chatted and laughed gayly with Francis Barold, as she approached the house; and after his departure she moved to and fro with a freedom not habitual to her.

"He has been making himself agreeable to her," said my lady, with grim pleasure. "He can do it if he chooses; and he is just the man to please a girl, — good-looking, and with a fine, domineering air."

"How did you enjoy yourself?" she asked.

"Very much," said Lucia; "never more, thank you."

"Oh!" ejaculated my lady. "And which of her smart New-York gowns did Miss Octavia Bassett wear?"

They were at the dinner-table; and, instead of looking down at her soup, Lucia looked quietly and steadily across the table at her grandmother.

"She wore a very pretty one," she said: "it was pale fawn-color, and fitted her like a glove. She made me feel very old-fashioned and badly dressed."

Lady Theobald laid down her spoon.

"She made you feel old-fashioned and badly dressed, — you!"

"Yes," responded Lucia: "she always does. I wonder what she thinks of the things we wear in Slowbridge." And she even went to the length of smiling a little.

"What *she* thinks of what is worn in Slowbridge!" Lady Theobald ejaculated. "She! may I ask what weight the opinion of a young woman from America — from Nevada — is supposed to have in Slowbridge?"

Lucia took a spoonful of soup in a leisurely manner.

"I don't think it is supposed to have any; but — but I don't think she minds that. I feel as if I shouldn't if I were in her place. I have always thought her very lucky."

"You have thought her lucky!" cried my lady. "You have envied a Nevada young woman, who dresses like an actress, and loads herself with jewels like a barbarian? A girl whose conduct toward men is of a character to — to chill one's blood!"

"They admire her," said Lucia simply, "more than they admire Lydia Egerton, and more than they admire me."

"Do *you* admire her?" demanded my lady.

"Yes, grandmamma," replied Lucia courageously. "I think I do."

Never had my lady been so astounded in her life. For a moment she could scarcely speak. When she recovered herself she pointed to the door.

"Go to your room," she commanded. "This is American freedom of speech, I suppose. Go to your room."

Lucia rose obediently. She could not help wondering what her ladyship's course would be if she had the hardihood to disregard her order. She really looked quite capable of carrying it out forcibly herself. When the girl stood at her bedroom window, a few minutes later, her cheeks were burning and her hands trembling.

"I am afraid it was very badly done," she said to herself. "I am sure it was; but — but it will be a kind of practice. I was in such a hurry to try if I were equal to it, that I didn't seem to balance things quite rightly. I ought to have waited until I had more reason to speak out. Perhaps there wasn't enough reason then, and I was more aggressive than I ought to have been. Octavia is never aggressive. I wonder if I was at all pert. I don't think Octavia ever means to be pert. I felt a little as if I meant to be pert. I must learn to balance myself, and only be cool and frank."

Then she looked out of the window, and reflected a little.

"I was not so very brave, after all," she said, rather reluctantly. "I didn't tell her Mr. Burmistone was there. I daren't have done that. I am afraid I *am* sly — that sounds sly, I am sure."

CHAPTER XVIII.

CONTRAST.

"LADY THEOBALD will put a stop to it," was the general remark. "It will certainly not occur again."

This was said upon the evening of the first gathering upon Miss Belinda's grass-plat, and at the same time it was prophesied that Mr. Francis Barold would soon go away.

But neither of the prophecies proved true. Mr. Francis Barold did *not* return to London; and, strange to say, Lucia was seen again and again playing croquet with Octavia Bassett, and was even known to spend evenings with her.

Perhaps it might be that an appeal made by Miss Belinda to her ladyship had caused her to allow of these things. Miss Belinda had, in fact, made a private call upon my lady, to lay her case before her.

"I feel so very timid about every thing,"

she said, almost with tears, "and so fearful of trusting myself, that I really find it quite a trial. The dear child has such a kind heart — I assure you she has a kind heart, dear Lady Theobald, — and is so innocent of any intention to do wrong — I am sure she is innocent, — that it seems cruel to judge her severely. If she had had the benefit of such training as dear Lucia's, I am convinced that her conduct would have been most exemplary. She sees herself that she has faults: I am sure she does. She said to me only last night, in that odd way of hers, — she had been sitting, evidently thinking deeply, for some minutes, — and she said, 'I wonder if I shouldn't be nicer if I were more like Lucia Gaston.' You see what turn her mind must have taken. She admires Lucia so much."

"Yesterday evening at dinner," said Lady Theobald severely, "Lucia informed me that *she* admired your niece. The feeling seems to be mutual."

Miss Belinda colored, and brightened visibly.

"Did she, indeed?" she exclaimed. "How

pleased Octavia will be to hear it! Did she, indeed?" Then, warned by a chilliness, and lack of response, in her ladyship's manner, she modified her delight, and became apologetic again. "These young people are more — are less critical than we are," she sighed. "Octavia's great prettiness" —

"I think," Lady Theobald interposed, "that Lucia has been taught to feel that the body is corruptible, and subject to decay, and that mere beauty is of small moment."

Miss Belinda sighed again.

"That is very true," she admitted deprecatingly; "very true indeed."

"It is to be hoped that Octavia's stay in Slowbridge will prove beneficial to her," said her ladyship in her most judicial manner. "The atmosphere is wholly unlike that which has surrounded her during her previous life."

"I am sure it will prove beneficial to her," said Miss Belinda eagerly. "The companionship of well-trained and refined young people cannot fail to be of use to her. Such a companion as Lucia would be, if you would kindly permit her to spend an evening with us now and then, would certainly improve and modify her greatly. Mr. Francis Barold is — is, I think, of the same opinion; at least, I fancied I gathered as much from a few words he let fall."

"Francis Barold?" repeated Lady Theobald. "And what did Francis Barold say?"

"Of course it was but very little," hesitated Miss Belinda; "but — but I could not help seeing that he was drawing comparisons, as it were. Octavia was teaching Mr. Poppleton to play croquet; and she was rather exhilarated, and perhaps exhibited more — freedom of manner, in an innocent way, — quite in an innocent, thoughtless way, — than is exactly customary; and I saw Mr. Barold glance from her to Lucia, who stood near; and when I said, 'You are thinking of the contrast between them,' he answered, 'Yes, they differ very greatly, it is true;' and of course I knew that my poor Octavia could not have the advantage in his eyes. She feels this herself, I know. She shocked me the other day, beyond expression, by telling me that she had asked him if he thought she was really fast, and that she was sure he did. Poor child! she evidently did not comprehend the dreadful significance of such terms."

"A man like Francis Barold does understand their significance," said Lady Theobald; "and it is to be deplored that your niece cannot be taught what her position in society will be if such a reputation attaches itself to her. The men of the present day fight shy of such characters."

This dread clause so impressed poor Miss Belinda by its solemnity, that she could not forbear repeating it to Octavia afterward, though it is to be regretted that it did not produce the effect she had hoped.

"Well, I must say," she observed, "that if some men fought a little shyer than they do, I shouldn't mind it. You always *do* have about half a dozen dangling around, who only bore you, and who will keep asking you to go to places, and sending you bouquets, and asking you to dance when they can't dance at all, and only tear your dress, and stand on your feet. If they would 'fight shy,' it would be splendid."

To Miss Belinda, who certainly had never been guilty of the indecorum of having any member of the stronger sex "dangling about" at all, this was very trying.

"My dear," she said, "don't say 'you always have;' it — it really seems to make it so personal."

Octavia turned around, and fixed her eyes wonderingly upon her blushing countenance. For a moment she made no remark, a marvellous thought shaping itself slowly in her mind.

"Aunt Belinda," she said at length, "did nobody ever" —

"Ah, no, my dear! No, no, I assure you!" cried Miss Belinda, in the greatest possible trepidation. "Ah, dear, no! Such — such things rarely — very rarely happen in — Slowbridge; and, besides, I couldn't possibly have thought of it. I couldn't, indeed!"

She was so overwhelmed with maidenly confusion at the appalling thought, that she did not recover herself for half an hour at least. Octavia, feeling that it would not be safe to pursue the subject, only uttered one word of comment, —

"Gracious!"

CHAPTER XIX.

AN EXPERIMENT.

MUCH to her own astonishment, Lucia found herself allowed new liberty. She was permitted to spend the afternoon frequently with Octavia; and on several occasions that young lady and Miss Bassett were invited to partake of tea at Oldclough in company with no other guest than Francis Barold.

"I don't know what it means, and I think it must mean something," said Lucia to Octavia; "but it is very pleasant. I never was allowed to be so intimate with any one before."

"Perhaps," suggested Octavia sagely, "she thinks, that, if you see me often enough, you will get sick of me, and it will be a lesson to you."

"The more I see of you," answered Lucia with a serious little air, "the fonder I am of you. I understand you better. You are not at all like what I thought you at first, Octavia."

"But I don't know that there's much to understand in me."

"There is a great deal to understand in you," she replied. "You are a puzzle to me often. You seem so frank, and yet one knows so little about you after all. For instance," Lucia went on, "who would imagine that you are so affectionate?"

"Am I affectionate?" she asked.

"Yes," answered Lucia: "I am sure you are very affectionate. I have found it out gradually. You would suffer things for any one you loved."

Octavia thought the matter over.

"Yes," she said at length, "I would."

"You are very fond of Miss Bassett," proceeded Lucia, as if arraigning her at the bar of justice. "You are *very* fond of your father; and I am sure there are other people you are very fond of — *very* fond of indeed."

Octavia pondered seriously again.

"Yes, there are," she remarked; "but no one would care about them here, and so I'm not going to make a fuss. You don't want to make a fuss over people you l-like."

"*You* don't," said Lucia. "You are like Francis Barold in one way, but you are altogether different in another. Francis Barold does not wish to show emotion; and he is so determined to hedge himself around, that one can't help suspecting that he is always guarding himself against one. He seems always to be resenting any interference; but you do not appear to care at all, and so it is not natural that one should suspect you. I did not suspect you."

"What do you suspect me of now?"

"Of thinking a great deal," answered Lucia affectionately. "And of being very clever and very good."

Octavia was silent for a few moments.

"I think," she said after the pause, — "I think you'll find out that it's a mistake."

"No, I shall not," returned Lucia, quite glowing with enthusiasm. "And I know I shall learn a great deal from you."

This was such a startling proposition that Octavia felt decidedly uncomfortable. She flushed rosy red.

"I'm the one who ought to learn things, I think," she said. "I'm always doing things that frighten aunt Belinda, and you know how the rest regard me."

"Octavia," said Lucia, very naïvely indeed, "suppose we try to help each other. If you will tell me when I am wrong, I will try to — to have the courage to tell you. That will be good practice for me. What I want most is courage and frankness, and I am sure it will take courage to make up my mind to tell you of your — of your mistakes."

Octavia regarded her with mingled admiration and respect.

"I think that's a splendid idea," she said.

"Are you sure," faltered Lucia, "are you sure you won't mind the things I may have to say? Really, they are quite little things in themselves — hardly worth mentioning " —

"Tell me one of them, right now," said Octavia, point-blank.

"Oh, no!" exclaimed Lucia, starting. "I'd rather not — just now."

"Well," commented Octavia, "that sounds as if they must be pretty unpleasant. Why don't you want to? They will be quite as bad to-morrow. And to refuse to tell me one is a bad beginning. It looks as if you were frightened; and it isn't good practice for you to be frightened at such a little thing."

Lucia felt convicted. She made an effort to regain her composure.

"No, it is not," she said. "But that is always the way. I am continually telling myself that I *will* be courageous and candid; and, the first time any thing happens, I fail. I *will* tell you one thing."

She stopped short here, and looked at Octavia guiltily.

"It is something — I think I would do if — if I were in your place," Lucia stammered. "A very little thing indeed."

"Well?" remarked Octavia anxiously.

Lucia lost her breath, caught it again, and proceeded cautiously, and with blushes at her own daring.

"If I were in your place," she said, "I think — that, perhaps — only perhaps, you know — I would not wear — my hair — *quite* so low down — over my forehead."

Octavia sprang from her seat, and ran to the pier-glass over the mantle. She glanced at the reflection of her own startled, pretty face, and then, putting her hand up to the soft blonde "bang" which met her brows, turned to Lucia.

"Isn't it becoming?" she asked breathlessly.

"Oh, yes!" Lucia answered. "Very."

Octavia started.

"Then, why wouldn't you wear it?" she cried. "What do you mean?"

Lucia felt her position truly a delicate one. She locked her hands, and braced herself; but she blushed vividly.

"It may sound rather silly when I tell you why, Octavia," she said; "but I really do think it is a sort of reason. You know, in those absurd pictures of actresses, bangs always seem to be the principal feature. I saw some in the shop-windows when I went to Harriford with grandmamma. And they were such dreadful women, — some of them, — and had so very few clothes on, that I can't help thinking I shouldn't like to look like them, and " —

"Does it make me look like them?."

"Oh, very little!" answered Lucia; "very little indeed, of course; but"—

"But it's the same thing after all," put in Octavia. "That's what you mean."

"It is so very little," faltered Lucia, "that — that perhaps it isn't a reason."

Octavia looked at herself in the glass again.

"It isn't a very good reason," she remarked, "but I suppose it will do."

She paused, and looked Lucia in the face.

"I don't think that's a little thing," she said. "To be told you look like an *opéra bouffe* actress."

"I did not mean to say so," cried Lucia, filled with the most poignant distress. "I beg your pardon, indeed — I — oh, dear! I was afraid you wouldn't like it. I felt that it was taking a great liberty."

"I don't like it," answered Octavia; "but that can't be helped. I didn't exactly suppose I should. But I wasn't going to say any thing about *your* hair when *I* began," glancing at poor Lucia's coiffure, "though I suppose I might."

"You might say a thousand things about

AN EXPERIMENT.

it!" cried Lucia piteously. "I know that mine is not only in bad taste, but it is ugly and unbecoming."

"Yes," said Octavia cruelly, "it is."

"And yours is neither the one nor the other," protested Lucia. "You know I told you it was pretty, Octavia."

Octavia walked over to the table, upon which stood Miss Belinda's work-basket, and took therefrom a small and gleaming pair of scissors, returning to the mantle-glass with them.

"How short shall I cut it?" she demanded.

"Oh!" exclaimed Lucia, "don't, don't!"

For answer, Octavia raised the scissors, and gave a snip. It was a savage snip, and half the length and width of her love-locks fell on the mantle; then she gave another snip, and the other half fell.

Lucia scarcely dared to breathe.

For a moment Octavia stood gazing at herself, with pale face and dilated eyes. Then suddenly the folly of the deed she had done seemed to reveal itself to her.

"Oh!" she cried out. "Oh, how diabolical it looks!"

She turned upon Lucia.

"Why did you make me do it?" she exclaimed. "It's all your fault — every bit of it;" and, flinging the scissors to the other end of the room, she threw herself into a chair, and burst into tears.

Lucia's anguish of mind was almost more than she could bear. For at least three minutes she felt herself a criminal of the deepest dye; after the three minutes had elapsed, however, she began to reason, and called to mind the fact that she was failing as usual under her crisis.

"This is being a coward again," she said to herself. "It is worse than to have said nothing. It is true that she will look more refined, now one can see a little of her forehead; and it is cowardly to be afraid to stand firm when I really think so. I — yes, I will say something to her."

"Octavia," she began aloud, "I am sure you are making a mistake again." This as decidedly as possible, which was not very decidedly. "You — you look very much — nicer."

"I look *ghastly!*" said Octavia, who began to feel rather absurd.

AN EXPERIMENT. 181

"You do not. Your forehead — you have the prettiest forehead I ever saw, Octavia," said Lucia eagerly; "and your eyebrows are perfect. I — wish you would look at yourself again."

Rather to her surprise, Octavia began to laugh under cover of her handkerchief: reaction had set in, and, though the laugh was a trifle hysterical, it was still a laugh. Next she gave her eyes a final little dab, and rose to go to the glass again. She looked at herself, touched up the short, waving fringe left on her forehead, and turned to Lucia, with a resigned expression.

"Do you think that any one who was used to seeing it the other way would — would think I looked horrid?" she inquired anxiously.

"They would think you prettier, — a great deal," Lucia answered earnestly. "Don't you know, Octavia, that nothing could be really unbecoming to you? You have that kind of face."

For a few seconds Octavia seemed to lose herself in thought of a speculative nature.

"Jack always said so," she remarked at length.

"Jack!" repeated Lucia timidly.

Octavia roused herself, and smiled with candid sweetness.

"He is some one I knew in Nevada," she explained. "He worked in father's mine once."

"You must have known him very well," suggested Lucia, somewhat awed.

"I did," she replied calmly. "Very well."

She tucked away her pocket-handkerchief in the jaunty pocket at the back of her basque, and returned to her chair. Then she turned again to Lucia.

"Well," she said, "I think you have found out that you *were* mistaken, haven't you, dear? Suppose you tell me of something else."

Lucia colored.

"No," she answered: "that is enough for to-day."

CHAPTER XX.

PECULIAR TO NEVADA.

WHETHER, or not, Lucia was right in accusing Octavia Bassett of being clever, and thinking a great deal, is a riddle which those who are interested in her must unravel as they read; but, whether the surmise was correct or incorrect, it seemed possible that she had thought a little after the interview. When Barold saw her next, he was struck by a slight but distinctly definable change he recognized in her dress and coiffure. Her pretty hair had a rather less "professional" appearance: he had the pleasure of observing, for the first time, how very white her forehead was, and how delicate the arch of her eyebrows; her dress had a novel air of simplicity, and the diamond rings were nowhere to be seen.

"She's better dressed than usual," he said to himself. "And she's always well dressed,

— rather too well dressed, fact is, for a place like this. This sort of thing is in better form, under the circumstances."

It was so much "better form," and he so far approved of it, that he quite thawed, and was very amiable and very entertaining indeed.

Octavia was entertaining too. She asked several most interesting questions.

"Do you think," she inquired, "that it is bad taste to wear diamonds?"

"My mother wears them — occasionally."

"Have you any sisters?"

"No."

"Any cousins — as young as I am?"

"Ya-as."

"Do they wear them?"

"I must admit," he replied, "that they don't. In the first place, you know, they haven't any; and, in the second, I am under the impression that Lady Beauchamp — their mamma, you know — wouldn't permit it if they had."

"Wouldn't permit it!" said Octavia. "I suppose they always do as she tells them?"

He smiled a little.

"They would be very courageous young women if they didn't," he remarked.

"What would she do if they tried it?" she inquired. "She couldn't beat them."

"They will never try it," he answered dryly. "And though I have never seen her beat them, or heard their lamentations under chastisement, I should not like to say that Lady Beauchamp could not do any thing. She is a very determined person — for a gentlewoman."

Octavia laughed.

"You are joking," she said.

"Lady Beauchamp is a serious subject for jokes," he responded. "My cousins think so, at least."

"I wonder if she is as bad as Lady Theobald," Octavia reflected aloud. "She says I have no right to wear diamonds at all until I am married. But I don't mind Lady Theobald," she added, as a cheerful afterthought. "I am not fond enough of her to care about what she says."

"Are you fond of any one?" Barold inquired, speaking with a languid air, but at the same time glancing at her with some slight interest from under his eyelids.

"Lucia says I am," she returned, with the calmness of a young person who wished to regard the matter from an unembarrassed point of view. "Lucia says I am affectionate."

"Ah!" deliberately. "Are you?"

She turned, and looked at him serenely.

"Should *you* think so?" she asked.

This was making such a personal matter of the question, that he did not exactly enjoy it. It was certainly not "good form" to pull a man up in such cool style.

"Really," he replied, "I — ah — have had no opportunity of judging."

He had not the slightest intention of being amusing, but to his infinite disgust he discovered as soon as he spoke that she was amused. She laughed outright, and evidently only checked herself because he looked so furious. In consideration for his feelings she assumed an air of mild but preternatural seriousness.

"No," she remarked, "that is true: you haven't, of course."

He was silent. He did not enjoy being amusing at all, and he made no pretence of appearing to submit to the indignity calmly.

She bent forward a little.

"Ah!" she exclaimed, "you are mad again — I mean, you are vexed. I am always vexing you."

There was a hint of appeal in her voice, which rather pleased him; but he had no intention of relenting at once.

"I confess I am at a loss to know why you laughed," he said.

"Are you," she asked, "really?" letting her eyes rest upon him anxiously for a moment. Then she actually gave vent to a little sigh. "We look at things so differently, that's it," she said.

"I suppose it is," he responded, still chillingly.

In spite of this, she suddenly assumed a comparatively cheerful aspect. A happy thought occurred to her.

"Lucia would beg your pardon," she said. "I am learning good manners from Lucia. Suppose I beg your pardon."

"It is quite unnecessary," he replied.

"Lucia wouldn't think so," she said. "And why shouldn't I be as well-behaved as Lucia? I beg your pardon."

He felt rather absurd, and yet somewhat mollified. She had a way of looking at him, sometimes, when she had been unpleasant, which rather soothed him. In fact, he had found of late, a little to his private annoyance, that it was very easy for her either to soothe or disturb him.

And now, just as Octavia had settled down into one of the prettiest and least difficult of her moods, there came a knock at the front door, which, being answered by Mary Anne, was found to announce the curate of St. James.

Enter, consequently, the Rev. Arthur Poppleton, — blushing, a trifle timorous perhaps, but happy beyond measure to find himself in Miss Belinda's parlor again, with Miss Belinda's niece.

Perhaps the least possible shade of his joyousness died out when he caught sight of Mr. Francis Barold, and certainly Mr. Francis Barold was not at all delighted to see him.

"What does the fellow want?" that gentleman was saying inwardly. "What does he come simpering and turning pink here for? Why doesn't he go and see some of his old women, and read tracts to them? That's *his* business."

Octavia's manner toward her visitor formed a fresh grievance for Barold. She treated the curate very well indeed. She seemed glad to see him, she was wholly at her ease with him, she made no trying remarks to him, she never stopped to fix her eyes upon him in that inexplicable style, and she did not laugh when there seemed nothing to laugh at. She was so gay and good-humored that the Rev. Arthur Poppleton beamed and flourished under her treatment, and forgot to change color, and even ventured to talk a good deal, and make divers quite presentable little jokes.

"I should like to know," thought Barold, growing sulkier as the others grew merrier, — "I should like to know what she finds so interesting in him, and why she chooses to treat him better than she treats me; for she certainly does treat him better."

It was hardly fair, however, that he should complain; for, at times, he was treated extremely well, and his intimacy with Octavia progressed quite rapidly. Perhaps, if the truth were told, it was always himself who was the first means of checking it, by some suddenly prudent instinct which led him to feel that perhaps he was in rather a delicate position, and had better not indulge in too much of a good thing. He had not been an eligible and unimpeachable desirable *parti* for ten years without acquiring some of that discretion which is said to be the better part of valor. The matter-of-fact air with which Octavia accepted his attentions caused him to pull himself up sometimes. If he had been Brown, or Jones, or even Robinson, she could not have appeared to regard them as more entirely natural. When — he had gone so far, once or twice — he had deigned to make a more than usually agreeable speech to her, it was received with none of that charming sensitive tremor to which he was accustomed. Octavia neither blushed, nor dropped her eyes.

It did not add to Barold's satisfaction to find her as cheerful and ready to be amused by a mild little curate, who blushed and stammered, and was neither brilliant, graceful, nor distinguished. Could not Octavia see the wide difference between the two?

Regarding the matter in this light, and watching Octavia as she encouraged her visitor, and laughed at his jokes, and never once tripped him up by asking him a startling question, did not, as already has been said, improve Mr. Francis Barold's temper; and, by the time his visit was over, he had lapsed into his coldest and most haughty manner. As soon as Miss Belinda entered, and engaged Mr. Poppleton for a moment, he rose, and crossed the little room to Octavia's side.

"I must bid you good-afternoon," he said.

Octavia did not rise.

"Sit down a minute, while aunt Belinda is talking about red-flannel nightcaps and lumbago," she said. "I wanted to ask you something. By the way, what *is* lumbago?"

"Is that what you wished to ask me?" he inquired stiffly.

"No. I just thought of that. Have you ever had it? and what is it like? All the old people in Slowbridge have it, and they tell you all about it when you go to see them.

Aunt Belinda says so. What I wanted to ask you was different"—

"Possibly Miss Bassett might be able to tell you," he remarked.

"About the lumbago? Well, perhaps she might. I'll ask her. Do you think it bad taste in *me* to wear diamonds?"

She said this with the most delightful seriousness, fixing her eyes upon him with her very prettiest look of candid appeal, as if it were the most natural thing in the world that she should apply to him for information. He felt himself faltering again. How white that bit of forehead was! How soft that blonde, waving fringe of hair! What a lovely shape her eyes were, and how large and clear as she raised them!

"Why do you ask *me?*" he inquired.

"Because I think you are an unprejudiced person. Lady Theobald is not. I have confidence in you. Tell me."

There was a slight pause.

"Really," he said, after it, "I can scarcely believe that my opinion can be of any value in your eyes. I am — can only tell you that it is hardly customary in — an — in England for young people to wear a profusion of ornament."

"I wonder if I wear a profusion."

"You don't need any," he condescended. "You are too young, and — all that sort of thing."

She glanced down at her slim, unringed hands for a moment, her expression quite thoughtful.

"Lucia and I almost quarrelled the other day," she said — "at least, I almost quarrelled. It isn't so nice to be told of things, after all. I must say I don't like it as much as I thought I should."

He kept his seat longer than he had intended; and, when he rose to go, the Rev. Arthur Poppleton was shaking hands with Miss Belinda, and so it fell out that they left the house together.

"You know Miss Octavia Bassett well, I suppose," remarked Barold, with condescension, as they passed through the gate. "You clergymen are fortunate fellows."

"I wish that others knew her as well, sir," said the little gentleman, kindling. "I wish they knew her — her generosity and kindness of heart and ready sympathy with misfortune!"

"Ah!" commented Mr. Barold, twisting his mustache with somewhat of an incredulous air. This was not at all the sort of thing he had expected to hear. For his own part, it would not have occurred to him to suspect her of the possession of such desirable and orthodox qualities.

"There are those who — misunderstand her," cried the curate, warming with his subject, "who misunderstand, and — yes, and apply harsh terms to her innocent gayety and freedom of speech: if they knew her as I do, they would cease to do so."

"I should scarcely have thought " — began Barold.

"There are many who scarcely think it, — if you will pardon my interrupting you," said the curate. "I think they would scarcely believe it if I felt at liberty to tell them, which I regret to say I do not. I am almost breaking my word in saying what I cannot help saying to yourself. The poor under my care are better off since she came, and there are some who have seen her more than once, though she did not go as a teacher or to reprove them for faults; and her way of doing what she did was new to them, and perhaps much less serious than they were accustomed to, and they liked it all the better."

"Ah!" commented Barold again. "Flannel under-garments, and — that sort of thing."

"No," with much spirit, "not at all, sir; but what, as I said, they liked much better. It is not often they meet a beautiful creature who comes among them with open hands, and the natural, ungrudging way of giving which she has. Sometimes they are at a loss to understand, as well as the rest. They have been used to what is narrower and more — more exacting."

"They have been used to Lady Theobald," observed Barold, with a faint smile.

"It would not become me to — to mention Lady Theobald in any disparaging manner," replied the curate; "but the best and most charitable among us do not always carry out our good intentions in the best way. I dare say Lady Theobald would consider Miss

Octavia Bassett too readily influenced and too lavish."

"She is as generous with her money as with her diamonds perhaps," said Barold. "Possibly the quality is peculiar to Nevada. We part here, Mr. Poppleton, I believe. Good-morning."

CHAPTER XXI.

LORD LANSDOWNE.

ONE morning in the following week Mrs. Burnham attired herself in her second-best black silk, and, leaving the Misses Burnham practising diligently, turned her steps toward Oldclough Hall. Arriving there, she was ushered into the blue drawing-room by Dobson, in his character of footman; and in a few minutes Lucia appeared.

When Mrs. Burnham saw her, she assumed a slight air of surprise.

"Why, my dear," she said, as she shook hands, "I should scarcely have known you."

And, though this was something of an exaggeration, there was some excuse for the exclamation. Lucia was looking very charming, and several changes might be noted in her attire and appearance. The ugly twist had disappeared from her delicate head; and in its place were soft, loose waves and light puffs; she had even ventured on allowing a few ringed locks to stray on to her forehead; her white morning-dress no longer wore the trade-mark of Miss Chickie, but had been remodelled by some one of more taste.

"What a pretty gown, my dear!" said Mrs. Burnham, glancing at it curiously. "A Watteau plait down the back — isn't it a Watteau plait? — and little ruffles down the front, and pale pink bows. It is quite like some of Miss Octavia Bassett's dresses, only not so over-trimmed."

"I do not think Octavia's dresses would seem over-trimmed if she wore them in London or Paris," said Lucia bravely. "It is only because we are so very quiet, and dress so little in Slowbridge, that they seem so."

"And your hair!" remarked Mrs. Burnham. "You drew your idea of that from some style of hers, I suppose. Very becoming, indeed. Well, well! And how does Lady Theobald like all this, my dear?"

"I am not sure that" — Lucia was beginning, when her ladyship interrupted her by entering.

"My dear Lady Theobald," cried her visitor, rising, "I hope you are well. I have just been complimenting Lucia upon her pretty dress, and her new style of dressing her hair. Miss Octavia Bassett has been giving her the benefit of her experience, it appears. We have not been doing her justice. Who would have believed that she had come from Nevada to improve us?"

"Miss Octavia Bassett," said my lady sonorously, "has come from Nevada to teach our young people a great many things, — new fashions in duty, and demeanor, and respect for their elders. Let us hope they will be benefited."

"If you will excuse me, grandmamma," said Lucia, speaking in a soft, steady voice, "I will go and write the letters you wished written."

"Go," said my lady with majesty; and, having bidden Mrs. Burnham good-morning, Lucia went.

If Mrs. Burnham had expected any explanation of her ladyship's evident displeasure, she was doomed to disappointment. That excellent and rigorous gentlewoman had a stern sense of dignity, which forbade her condescending to the confidential weakness of mere ordinary mortals. Instead of referring to Lucia, she broached a more commonplace topic.

"I hope your rheumatism does not threaten you again, Mrs. Burnham," she remarked.

"I am very well, thank you, my dear," said Mrs. Burnham; "so well, that I am thinking quite seriously of taking the dear girls to the garden-party, when it comes off."

"To the garden-party!" repeated her ladyship. "May I ask who thinks of giving a garden-party in Slowbridge?"

"It is no one in Slowbridge," replied this lady cheerfully. "Some one who lives a little out of Slowbridge, — Mr. Burmistone, my dear Lady Theobald, at his new place."

"Mr. Burmistone!"

"Yes, my dear; and a most charming affair it is to be, if we are to believe all we hear. Surely you have heard something of it from Mr. Barold."

"Mr. Barold has not been to Oldclough for several days."

"Then, he will tell you when he comes; for I suppose he has as much to do with it as Mr. Burmistone."

"I have heard before," announced my lady, "of men of Mr. Burmistone's class securing the services of persons of established position in society when they wished to spend their money upon entertainments; but I should scarcely have imagined that Francis Barold would have allowed himself to be made a party to such a transaction."

"But," put in Mrs. Burnham rather eagerly, "it appears that Mr. Burmistone is not such an obscure person, after all. He is an Oxford man, and came off with honors: he is quite a well-born man, and gives this entertainment in honor of his friend and relation, Lord Lansdowne."

"Lord Lansdowne!" echoed her ladyship, sternly.

"Son of the Marquis of Lauderdale, whose wife was Lady Honora Erroll."

"Did Mr. Burmistone give you this information?" asked Lady Theobald with ironic calmness.

Mrs. Burnham colored never so faintly.

"I — that is to say — there is a sort of acquaintance between one of my maids and the butler at the Burmistone place; and, when the girl was doing Lydia's hair, she told her the story. Lord Lansdowne and his father are quite fond of Mr. Burmistone, it is said."

"It seems rather singular to my mind that we should not have known of this before."

"But how should we learn? We none of us know Lord Lansdowne, or even the marquis. I think he is only a second or third cousin. We are a little — just a little *set* in Slowbridge, you know, my dear: at least, I have thought so sometimes lately."

"I must confess," remarked my lady, "that *I* have not regarded the matter in that light."

"That is because you have a better right to — to be a little set than the rest of us," was the amiable response.

Lady Theobald did not disclaim the privilege. She felt the sentiment an extremely correct one. But she was not very warm in her manner during the remainder of the call; and, incongruous as such a statement may appear, it must be confessed that she felt that Miss Octavia Bassett must have something to do with these defections on all sides, and that garden-parties, and all such swervings from established Slowbridge custom, were the natural result of Nevada frivolity and freedom of manners. It may be that she felt remotely that even Lord Lansdowne and the Marquis of Lauderdale were to be referred to the same reprehensible cause, and that, but for Octavia Bassett, Mr. Burmistone would not have been educated at Oxford and have come off with honors, and have turned out to be related to respectable people, but would have remained in appropriate obscurity.

"I suppose," she said afterward to Lucia, "that your friend Miss Octavia Bassett is in Mr. Burmistone's confidence, if no one else has been permitted to have that honor. I have no doubt *she* has known of this approaching entertainment for some weeks."

"I do not know, grandmamma," replied Lucia, putting her letters together, and gaining color as she bent over them. She was wondering, with inward trepidation, what her ladyship would say if she knew the whole truth, — if she knew that it was her granddaughter, and not Octavia Bassett, who enjoyed Mr. Burmistone's confidence.

"Ah!" she thought, "how could I ever dare to tell her?"

The same day Francis Barold sauntered up to pay them a visit; and then, as Mrs. Burnham had prophesied, Lady Theobald heard all she wished to hear, and, indeed, a great deal more.

"What is this I am told of Mr. Burmistone, Francis?" she inquired. "That he intends to give a garden-party, and that Lord Lansdowne is to be one of the guests, and that he has caused it to be circulated that they are cousins."

"That Lansdowne has caused it to be circulated — or Burmistone?"

"It is scarcely likely that Lord Lansdowne"—

"Beg pardon," he interrupted, fixing his single glass dexterously in his right eye, and gazing at her ladyship through it. "Can't see why Lansdowne should object. Fact is, he is a great deal fonder of Burmistone than relations usually are of each other. Now, I often find that kind of thing a bore; but Lansdowne doesn't seem to. They were at school together, it seems, and at Oxford too; and Burmistone is supposed to have behaved pretty well towards Lansdowne at one time, when he was rather a wild fellow — so the father and mother say. As to Burmistone 'causing it to be circulated,' that sort of thing is rather absurd. The man isn't a cad, you know."

"Pray don't say 'you know,' Francis," said her ladyship. "I know very little but what I have chanced to see, and I must confess I have not been prepossessed in Mr. Burmistone's favor. Why did he not choose to inform us " —

"That he was Lord Lansdowne's second cousin, and knew the Marquis of Lauderdale, grandmamma?" broke in Lucia, with very pretty spirit. "Would that have prepossessed you in his favor? Would you have forgiven him for building the mills, on Lord Lansdowne's account? I — I wish I was related to a marquis," which was very bold indeed.

"May I ask," said her ladyship, in her most monumental manner, "when *you* became Mr. Burmistone's champion?"

CHAPTER XXII.

"YOU HAVE MADE IT LIVELIER."

WHEN she had become Mr. Burmistone's champion, indeed! She could scarcely have told when, unless, perhaps, she had fixed the date at the first time she had heard his name introduced at a high tea, with every politely opprobrious epithet affixed. She had defended him in her own mind then, and felt sure that he deserved very little that was said against him, and very likely nothing at all. And, the first time she had seen and spoken to him, she had been convinced that she had not made a mistake, and that he had been treated with cruel injustice. How kind he was, how manly, how clever, and how well he bore himself under the popular adverse criticism! She only wondered that anybody could be so blind and stupid and wilful as to assail him.

And if this had been the case in those

early days, imagine what she felt now, when — ah, well! — when her friendship had had time and opportunity to become a much deeper sentiment. Must it be confessed that she had seen Mr. Burmistone even oftener than Octavia and Miss Belinda knew of? Of course it had all been quite accidental; but it had happened that now and then, when she had been taking a quiet walk in the lanes about Oldclough, she had encountered a gentleman, who had dismounted, and led his horse by the bridle, as he sauntered by her side. She had always been very timid at such times, and had felt rather like a criminal; but Mr. Burmistone had not been timid at all, and would, indeed, as soon have met Lady Theobald as not, for which courage his companion admired him more than ever. It was not very long before to be with this hero re-assured her, and made her feel stronger and more self-reliant. She was never afraid to open her soft little heart to him, and show him innocently all its goodness, and ignorance of worldliness. She warmed and brightened under his kindly influence, and was often surprised in secret at her own simple readiness of wit and speech.

"It is odd that I am such a different girl when — when I am with you," she said to him one day. "I even make little jokes. I never should think of making even the tiniest joke before grandmamma. Somehow, she never seems quite to understand jokes. She never laughs at them. You always laugh, and I am sure it is very kind of you to encourage me so; but you must not encourage me too much, or I might forget, and make a little joke at dinner, and I think, if I did, she would choke over her soup."

Perhaps, when she dressed her hair, and adorned herself with pale pink bows and like appurtenances, this artful young person had privately in mind other beholders than Mrs. Burnham, and other commendation than that to be bestowed by that most excellent matron.

"Do you mind my telling you that you have put on an enchanted garment?" said Mr. Burmistone, the first time they met when she wore one of the old-new gowns. "I thought I knew before how" —

"I don't mind it at all," said Lucia, blushing brilliantly. "I rather like it. It rewards me for my industry. My hair is dressed in a new way. I hope you like that too. Grandmamma does not."

It had been Lady Theobald's habit to treat Lucia severely from a sense of duty. Her manner toward her had always rather the tone of implying that she was naturally at fault, and yet her ladyship could not have told wherein she wished the girl changed. In the good old school in which my lady had been trained, it was customary to regard young people as weak, foolish, and, if left to their own desires, frequently sinful. Lucia had not been left to her own desires. She had been taught to view herself as rather a bad case, and to feel that she was far from being what her relatives had a right to expect. To be thrown with a person who did not find her silly or dull or commonplace, was a new experience.

"If I had been clever," Lucia said once to Mr. Burmistone, — "if I had been clever, perhaps grandmamma would have been more satisfied with me. I have often wished I had been clever."

"If you had been a boy," replied Mr. Burmistone rather grimly, "and had squandered her money, and run into debt, and bullied her, you would have been her idol, and she would have pinched and starved herself to supply your highness's extravagance."

When the garden-party rumor began to take definite form, and there was no doubt as to Mr. Burmistone's intentions, a discussion arose at once, and went on in every genteel parlor. Would Lady Theobald allow Lucia to go? and, if she did not allow her, would not such a course appear very pointed indeed? It was universally decided that it would appear pointed, but that Lady Theobald would not mind that in the least, and perhaps would rather enjoy it than otherwise; and it was thought Lucia would not go. And it is very likely that Lucia would have remained at home, if it had not been for the influence of Mr. Francis Barold.

Making a call at Oldclough, he found his august relative in a very majestic mood, and she applied to him again for information.

"Perhaps," she said, "you may be able to tell me whether it is true that Belinda Bassett — *Belinda Bassett*," with emphasis, "has been invited by Mr. Burmistone to assist him to receive his guests."

"Yes, it is true," was the reply: "I think I advised it myself. Burmistone is fond of her. They are great friends. Man needs a woman at such times."

"And he chose Belinda Bassett?"

"In the first place, he is on friendly terms with her, as I said before," replied Barold; "in the second, she's just what he wants — well-bred, kind-hearted, not likely to make rows, *et cœtera*." There was a slight pause before he finished, adding quietly, "He's not the man to submit to being refused — Burmistone."

Lady Theobald did not reply, or raise her eyes from her work: she knew he was looking at her with calm fixedness, through the glass he held in its place so cleverly; and she detested this more than any thing else, perhaps because she was invariably quelled by it, and found she had nothing to say.

He did not address her again immediately,

but turned to Lucia, dropping the eyeglass, and resuming his normal condition.

"You will go, of course?" he said.

Lucia glanced across at my lady.

"I — do not know. Grandmamma" —

"Oh!" interposed Barold, "you must go. There is no reason for your refusing the invitation, unless you wish to imply something unpleasant — which is, of course, out of the question."

"But there may be reasons" — began her ladyship.

"Burmistone is my friend," put in Barold, in his coolest tone; "and I am your relative, which would make my position in his house a delicate one, if he has offended you."

When Lucia saw Octavia again, she was able to tell her that they had received invitations to the *fête*, and that Lady Theobald had accepted them.

"She has not spoken a word to me about it, but she has accepted them," said Lucia. "I don't quite understand her lately, Octavia. She must be very fond of Francis Barold. He never gives way to her in the least, and she always seems to submit to him. I know she would not have let me go, if he had not insisted on it, in that taking-it-for-granted way of his."

Naturally Mr. Burmistone's *fête* caused great excitement. Miss Chickie was never so busy in her life, and there were rumors that her feelings had been outraged by the discovery that Mrs. Burnham had sent to Harriford for costumes for her daughters.

"Slowbridge is changing, mem," said Miss Chickie, with brilliant sarcasm. "Our ladies is led in their fashions by a Nevada young person. We're improving most rapid — more rapid than I'd ever have dared to hope. Do you prefer a frill, or a flounce, mem?"

Octavia was in great good spirits at the prospect of the gayeties in question. She had been in remarkably good spirits for some weeks. She had received letters from Nevada, containing good news she said. Shares had gone up again; and her father had almost settled his affairs, and it would not be long before he would come to England. She looked so exhilarated over the matter, that Lucia felt a little aggrieved.

"Will you be so glad to leave us, Octavia?" she asked. "We shall not be so glad to let you go. We have grown very fond of you."

"I shall be sorry to leave you, and aunt Belinda is going with us. You don't expect me to be very fond of Slowbridge, do you, and to be sorry I can't take Mrs. Burnham — and the rest?"

Barold was present when she made this speech, and it rather rankled.

"Am I one of 'the rest'?" he inquired, the first time he found himself alone with her. He was sufficiently piqued to forget his usual *hauteur* and discretion.

"Would you like to be?" she said.

"Oh! Very much — very much — naturally," he replied severely.

They were standing near a rose-bush in the garden; and she plucked a rose, and regarded it with deep interest.

"Well," she said, next, "I must say I think I shouldn't have had such a good time if you hadn't been here. You have made it livelier."

"Tha-anks," he remarked. "You are most kind."

"Oh!" she answered, "it's true. If it wasn't, I shouldn't say it. You and Mr. Burmistone and Mr. Poppleton have certainly made it livelier."

He went home in such a bad humor that his host, who was rather happier than usual, commented upon his grave aspect at dinner.

"You look as if you had heard ill news, old fellow," he said. "What's up?"

"Oh, nothing!" he was answered sardonically; "nothing whatever — unless that I have been rather snubbed by a young lady from Nevada."

"Ah!" with great seriousness: "that's rather cool, isn't it?"

"It's her little way," said Barold. "It seems to be one of the customs of Nevada."

In fact, he was very savage indeed. He felt that he had condescended a good deal lately. He seldom bestowed his time on women; and when he did so, at rare intervals, he chose those who would do the most honor to his taste at the least cost of trouble. And he was obliged to confess to himself that he had broken his rule in this case. Upon analyzing his motives and necessities, he found, that, after all, he must have extended his visit simply because he chose to see more of this young woman from Nevada, and that really, upon the whole, he had borne a good deal from her. Sometimes he had been much pleased with her, and very well entertained; but often enough — in fact, rather too often — she had made him exceedingly uncomfortable. Her manners were not what he was accustomed to: she did not consider that all men were not to be regarded from the same point of view. Perhaps he did not put into definite words the noble and patriotic sentiment that an Englishman was not to be regarded from the same point of view as an American, and that, though all this sort of thing might do with fellows in New York, it was scarcely what an Englishman would stand. Perhaps, as I say, he had not put this sentiment into words; but it is quite certain that it had been uppermost in his mind upon more occasions than one. As he thought their acquaintance over, this evening, he was rather severe upon Octavia. He even was roused so far as to condescend to talk her over with Burmistone.

"If she had been well brought up," he said, "she would have been a different creature."

"Very different, I have no doubt," said Burmistone thoughtfully. "When you say well brought up, by the way, do you mean brought up like your cousin, Miss Gaston?"

"There is a medium," said Barold loftily. "I regret to say Lady Theobald has not hit upon it."

"Well, as you say," commented Mr. Burmistone, "I suppose there is a medium."

"A charming wife she would make, for a man with a position to maintain," remarked Barold, with a short and somewhat savage laugh.

"Octavia Bassett?" queried Burmistone. "That's true. But I am afraid she wouldn't enjoy it — if you are supposing the man to be an Englishman, brought up in the regulation groove."

"Ah!" exclaimed Barold impatiently: "I was not looking at it from her point of view, but from his."

Mr. Burmistone slipped his hands in his pockets, and jingled his keys slightly, as he did once before in an earlier part of this narrative.

"Ah! from his," he repeated. "Not from hers. His point of view would differ from hers — naturally."

Barold flushed a little, and took his cigar from his mouth to knock off the ashes.

"A man is not necessarily a snob," he said, "because he is cool enough not to lose his head where a woman is concerned. You can't marry a woman who will make mistakes, and attract universal attention by her conduct."

"Has it struck you that Octavia Bassett would?" inquired Burmistone.

"She would do as she chose," said Barold petulantly. "She would do things which were unusual; but I was not referring to her in particular. Why should I?"

"Ah!" said Burmistone. "I only thought of her because it did not strike me that one would ever feel she had exactly blundered. She is not easily embarrassed. There is a *sang-froid* about her which carries things off."

"Ah!" deigned Barold: "she has *sang-froid* enough and to spare."

He was silent for some time afterward, and sat smoking later than usual. When he was about to leave the room for the night, he made an announcement for which his host was not altogether prepared.

"When the *fête* is over, my dear fellow," he said, "I must go back to London, and I shall be deucedly sorry to do it."

"Look here!" said Burmistone, "that's a new idea, isn't it?"

"No, an old one; but I have been putting the thing off from day to day. By Jove! I did not think it likely that I should put it off, the day I landed here."

And he laughed rather uneasily.

CHAPTER XXIII.

"MAY I GO?"

THE very day after this, Octavia opened the fourth trunk. She had had it brought down from the garret, when there came a summons on the door, and Lucia Gaston appeared.

Lucia was very pale; and her large, soft eyes wore a decidedly frightened look. She seemed to have walked fast, and was out of breath. Evidently something had happened.

"Octavia," she said, "Mr. Dugald Binnie is at Oldclough."

"Who is he?"

"He is my grand-uncle," explained Lucia tremulously. "He has a great deal of money. Grandmamma" — She stopped short, and colored, and drew her slight figure up. "I do not quite understand grandmamma, Octavia," she said. "Last night she came to my room to talk to me; and this morning she came again, and — oh!" she broke out indignantly, "how could she speak to me in such a manner!"

"What did she say?" inquired Octavia.

"She said a great many things," with great spirit. "It took her a long time to say them, and I do not wonder at it. It would have taken me a hundred years, if I had been in her place. I — I was wrong to say I did not understand her: I did — before she had finished."

"What did you understand?"

"She was afraid to tell me in plain words. — I never saw her afraid before, but she was afraid. She has been arranging my future for me, and it does not occur to her that I dare object. That is because she knows I am a coward, and despises me for it — and it is what I deserve. If I make the marriage she chooses, she thinks Mr. Binnie will leave me his money. I am to run after a man who does not care for me, and make myself attractive, in the hope that he will condescend to marry me because Mr. Binnie may leave me his money. Do you wonder that it took even Lady Theobald a long time to say that?"

"Well," remarked Octavia, "you won't do it, I suppose. I wouldn't worry. She wants you to marry Mr. Barold, I suppose."

Lucia started.

"How did you guess?" she exclaimed.

"Oh! I always knew it. I didn't guess." And she smiled ever so faintly. "That is one of the reasons why she loathes me so," she added.

Lucia thought deeply for a moment: she recognized, all at once, several things she had been mystified by before.

"Oh, it is! It is!" she said. "And she has thought of it all the time, when I never suspected her."

Octavia smiled a little again. Lucia sat thinking, her hands clasped tightly.

"I am glad I came here," she said, at length. "I *am* angry now, and I see things more clearly. If she had only thought of it because Mr. Binnie came, I could have forgiven her more easily; but she has been making coarse plans all the time, and treating me with contempt. Octavia," she added, turning upon her, with flushing cheeks and sparkling eyes, "I think that, for the first time in my life, I am in a passion,—a real passion. I think I shall never be afraid of her any more." Her delicate nostrils were dilated, she held her head up, her breath came fast. There was a hint of exultation in her tone. "Yes," she said, "I am in a passion. And I am not afraid of her at all. I will go home and tell her what I think."

And it is quite probable that she would have done so, but for a trifling incident which occurred before she reached her ladyship.

She walked very fast, after she left the house. She wanted to reach Oldclough before one whit of her anger cooled down; though, somehow, she felt quite sure, that, even when her anger died out, her courage would not take flight with it. Mr. Dugald Binnie had not proved to be a very fascinating person. He was an acrid, dictatorial old man: he contradicted Lady Theobald flatly every five minutes, and bullied his man-servant. But it was not against him that Lucia's indignation was aroused. She felt that Lady Theobald was quite capable of suggesting to him that Francis Barold would be a good match for her; and, if she had done so, it was scarcely his fault if he had accepted the idea. She understood now why she had been allowed to visit Octavia, and why divers other things had happened. She had been sent to walk with Francis Barold; he had been almost reproached when he had not called; perhaps her ladyship had been good enough to suggest to him that it was his duty to further her plans. She was as capable of that as of any thing else which would assist her to gain her point. The girl's cheeks grew hotter and hotter, her eyes brighter, at every step, because every step brought some new thought: her hands trembled, and her heart beat.

"I shall never be afraid of her again," she said, as she turned the corner into the road. "Never! never!"

And at that very moment a gentleman stepped out of the wood at her right, and stopped before her.

She started back, with a cry.

"Mr. Burmistone!" she said: "Mr. Burmistone!"

She wondered if he had heard her last words: she fancied he had. He took hold of her shaking little hand, and looked down at her excited face.

"I am glad I waited for you," he said, in the quietest possible tone. "Something is the matter."

She knew there would be no use in trying to conceal the truth, and she was not in the mood to make the effort. She scarcely knew herself.

She gave quite a fierce little laugh.

"I am angry!" she said. "You have never seen me angry before. I am on my way to my — to Lady Theobald."

He held her hand as calmly as before. He understood a great deal more than she could have imagined.

"What are you going to say to her?" he asked. She laughed again.

"I am going to ask her what she means. I am going to tell her she has made a mistake. I am going to prove to her that I am not such a coward, after all. I am going to tell her that I dare disobey her, — *that* is what I am going to say to her," she concluded decisively.

He held her hand rather closer.

"Let us take a stroll in the copse, and talk it over," he said. "It is deliciously cool there."

"I don't want to be cool," she said. But he drew her gently with him; and a few steps took them into the shade of the young oaks and pines, and there he paused.

"She has made you very angry?" he said.

And then, almost before she knew what she was doing, she was pouring forth the whole of her story, even more of it than she had told Octavia. She had not at all intended to do it; but she did it, nevertheless.

"I am to marry Mr. Francis Barold, if he will take me," she said, with a bitter little smile, — "Mr. Francis Barold, who is so much in love with me, as you know. His mother approves of the match, and sent him here to make love to me, which he has done, as you have seen. I have no money of my own; but, if I make a marriage which pleases him, Dugald Binnie will probably leave me his — which it is thought will be an inducement to my cousin, who needs one. If I marry him, or rather he marries me,

Lady Theobald thinks Mr. Binnie will be pleased. It does not even matter whether Francis is pleased or not, and of course I am out of the question; but it is hoped that it will please Mr. Binnie. The two ladies have talked it over, and decided the matter. I dare say they have offered me to Francis, who has very likely refused me, though perhaps he may be persuaded to relent in time, — if I am very humble, and he is shown the advantage of having Mr. Binnie's money added to his own, — but I have no doubt I shall have to be very humble indeed. That is what I learned from Lady Theobald last night, and it is what I am going to talk to her about. Is it enough to make one angry, do you think? is it enough?"

He did not tell her whether he thought it enough, or not. He looked at her with steady eyes.

"Lucia," he said, "I wish you would let *me* go and talk with Lady Theobald."

"You?" she said with a little start.

"Yes," he answered. "Let me go to her. Let me tell her, that, instead of marrying Francis Barold, you will marry *me*. If you will say yes to that, I think I can promise that you need never be afraid of her any more."

The fierce color died out of her cheeks, and the tears rushed to her eyes. She raised her face with a pathetic look.

"Oh!" she whispered, "you must be very sorry for me. I think you have been sorry for me from the first."

"I am desperately in love with you," he answered, in his quietest way. "I have been desperately in love with you from the first. May I go?"

She looked at him for a moment, incredulously. Then she faltered, —

"Yes."

She still looked up at him; and then, in spite of her happiness, or perhaps because of it, she suddenly began to cry softly, and forgot she had been angry at all, as he took her into his strong, kind arms.

CHAPTER XXIV.

THE GARDEN-PARTY.

THE morning of the garden-party arose bright and clear, and Slowbridge awakened in a great state of excitement. Miss Chickie, having worked until midnight that all her orders might be completed, was so overpowered by her labors as to have to take her tea and toast in bed.

At Oldclough varied sentiments prevailed. Lady Theobald's manner was chiefly distinguished by an implacable rigidity. She had chosen, as an appropriate festal costume, a funereal-black *moire antique*, enlivened by massive fringes and ornaments of jet; her jewelry being chains and manacles of the latter, which rattled as she moved, with a sound somewhat suggestive of bones.

Mr. Dugald Binnie, who had received an invitation, had as yet amiably forborne to say whether he would accept it, or not. He had

THE GARDEN-PARTY.

been out when Mr. Burmistone called, and had not seen him.

When Lady Theobald descended to breakfast, she found him growling over his newspaper; and he glanced up at her with a polite scowl.

"Going to a funeral?" he demanded.

"I accompany my granddaughter to this — this entertainment," her ladyship responded. "It is scarcely a joyous occasion, to my mind."

"No need to dress yourself like that, if it isn't," ejaculated Mr. Binnie. "Why don't you stay at home, if you don't want to go? Man's all right, isn't he? Once knew a man by the name of Burmistone, myself. One of the few decent fellows I've met. If I were sure this was the same man, I'd go myself. When I find a fellow who's neither knave nor fool, I stick to him. Believe I'll send to find out. Where's Lucia?"

What his opinion of Lucia was, it was difficult to discover. He had an agreeable habit of staring at her over the top of his paper, and over his dinner. The only time he had made any comment upon her, was the first time he saw her in the dress she had copied from Octavia's.

"Nice gown that," he blurted out: "didn't get it here, I'll wager."

"It's an old dress I remodelled," answered Lucia somewhat alarmed. "I made it myself."

"Doesn't look like it," he said gruffly.

Lucia had touched up another dress, and was very happy in the prospect of wearing it at the garden-party.

"Don't call on grandmamma until after Wednesday," she had said to Mr. Burmistone: "perhaps she wouldn't let me go. She will be very angry, I am sure."

"And you are not afraid?"

"No," she answered: "I am not afraid at all. I shall not be afraid again."

In fact, she had perfectly confounded her ladyship by her demeanor. She bore her fiercest glance without quailing in the least, or making any effort to evade it: under her most scathing comments she was composed and unmoved. On the first occasion of my lady's referring to her plans for her future, she received a blow which fairly stunned her. The girl rose from her chair, and looked her straight in the face unflinchingly, and with a suggestion of *hauteur* not easy to confront.

"I beg you will not speak to me of that again," she said: "I will not listen." And turning about, she walked out of the room.

"This," her ladyship had said in sepulchral tones, when she recovered her breath, "this is one of the results of Miss Octavia Bassett." And nothing more had been said on the subject since.

No one in Slowbridge was in more brilliant spirits than Octavia herself on the morning of the *fête*. Before breakfast Miss Belinda was startled by the arrival of another telegram, which ran as follows: —

"Arrived to-day, per 'Russia.' Be with you to-morrow evening. Friend with me.

"MARTIN BASSETT."

On reading this communication, Miss Belinda burst into floods of delighted tears.

"Dear, dear Martin," she wept; "to think that we should meet again! *Why* didn't he let us know he was on the way? I should have been so anxious that I should not have slept at all."

"Well," remarked Octavia, "I suppose that would have been an advantage."

Suddenly she approached Miss Belinda, kissed her, and disappeared out of the room as if by magic, not returning for a quarter of an hour, looking rather soft and moist and brilliant about the eyes when she did return.

Octavia was a marked figure upon the grounds at that garden-party.

"Another dress, my dear," remarked Mrs. Burnham. "And what a charming color she has, I declare! She is usually paler. Perhaps we owe this to Lord Lansdowne."

"Her dress is becoming, at all events," privately remarked Miss Lydia Burnham, whose tastes had not been consulted about her own.

"It is she who is becoming," said her sister: "it is not the dress so much, though her clothes always have a *look*, some way. She's prettier than ever to-day, and is enjoying herself."

She was enjoying herself. Mr. Francis Barold observed it rather gloomily as he stood apart. She was enjoying herself so much, that she did not seem to notice that he had avoided her, instead of going up to claim her attention. Half a dozen men were standing about her, and making themselves agreeable; and she was apparently quite equal to the emergencies of the occasion. The young men from Broadoaks had at once attached themselves to her train.

"I say, Barold," they had said to him, "why didn't you tell us about this? Jolly good fellow you are, to come mooning here for a couple of months, and keep it all to yourself."

And then had come Lord Lansdowne, who, in crossing the lawn to shake hands with his host, had been observed to keep his eye fixed upon one particular point.

"Burmistone," he said, after having spoken his first words, "who is that tall girl in white?"

And in ten minutes Lady Theobald, Mrs. Burnham, Mr. Barold, and divers others too numerous to mention, saw him standing at

Octavia's side, evidently with no intention of leaving it.

Not long after this Francis Barold found his way to Miss Belinda, who was very busy and rather nervous.

"Your niece is evidently enjoying herself," he remarked.

"Octavia is most happy to-day," answered Miss Belinda. "Her father will reach Slowbridge this evening. She has been looking forward to his coming with great anxiety."

"Ah!" commented Barold.

"Very few people understand Octavia," said Miss Belinda. "I'm not sure that I follow all her moods myself. She is more affectionate than people fancy. She — she has very pretty ways. I am very fond of her. She is not as frivolous as she appears to those who don't know her well."

Barold stood gnawing his mustache, and made no reply. He was not very comfortable. He felt himself ill-used by Fate, and rather wished he had returned to London from Broadoaks, instead of loitering in Slowbridge. He had amused himself at first, but in time he had been surprised to find his amusement lose something of its zest. He glowered across the lawn at the group under a certain beech-tree; and, as he did so, Octavia turned her face a little and saw him. She stood waving her fan slowly, and smiling at him in a calm way, which reminded him very much of the time he had first caught sight of her at Lady Theobald's high tea.

He condescended to saunter over the grass to where she stood. Once there, he proceeded to make himself as disagreeable as possible, in a silent and lofty way. He felt it only due to himself that he should. He did not approve at all of the manner in which Lansdowne kept by her.

"It's deucedly bad form on his part," he said mentally. "What does he mean by it?"

Octavia, on the contrary, did not ask what he meant by it. She chose to seem rather well entertained, and did not notice that she was being frowned down. There was no reason why she should not find Lord Lansdowne entertaining: he was an agreeable young fellow, with an inexhaustible fund of good spirits, and no nonsense about him.

He was fond of all pleasant novelty, and Octavia was a pleasant novelty. He had been thinking of paying a visit to America; and he asked innumerable questions concerning that country, all of which Octavia answered.

"I know half a dozen fellows who have been there," he said. "And they all enjoyed it tremendously."

"If you go to Nevada, you must visit the mines at Bloody Gulch," she said.

"Where?" he ejaculated. "I say, what a name! Don't deride my youth and ignorance, Miss Bassett."

"You can call it L'Argentville, if you would rather," she replied.

"I would rather try the other, thank you," he laughed. "It has a more hilarious sound. Will they despise me at Bloody Gulch, Miss Bassett? I never killed a man in my life."

Barold turned, and walked away, angry, and more melancholy than he could have believed.

"It is time I went back to London," he chose to put it. "The place begins to be deucedly dull."

"Mr. Francis Barold seems rather out of spirits," said Mrs. Burnham to Lady Theobald. "Lord Lansdowne interferes with his pleasure."

"I had not observed it," answered her ladyship. "And it is scarcely likely that Mr. Francis Barold would permit his pleasure to be interfered with, even by the son of the Marquis of Lauderdale."

But she glared at Barold as he passed, and beckoned to him.

"Where is Lucia?" she demanded.

"I saw her with Burmistone half an hour ago," he answered coldly. "Have you any message for my mother? I shall return to London to-morrow, leaving here early."

She turned quite pale. She had not counted upon this at all, and it was extremely inopportune.

"What has happened?" she asked rigidly.

He looked slightly surprised.

"Nothing whatever," he replied. "I have remained here longer than I intended."

She began to move the manacles on her right wrist. He made not the smallest profession of reluctance to go. She said, at last, —

"If you will find Lucia, you will oblige me."

She was almost uncivil to Miss Pilcher, who chanced to join her after he was gone. She had not the slightest intention of allowing her plans to be frustrated, and was only roused to fresh obstinacy by encountering indifference on one side and rebellion on the other. She had not brought Lucia up under her own eye for nothing. She had been disturbed of late, but by no means considered herself baffled. With the assistance of Mr. Dugald Binnie, she could certainly subdue Lucia, though Mr. Dugald Binnie had been of no great help so far. She would do her duty unflinchingly. In fact, she chose to persuade herself, that, if Lucia was brought to a proper frame of mind, there could be no real trouble with Francis Barold.

CHAPTER XXV.

"SOMEBODY ELSE."

But Barold did not make any very ardent search for Lucia. He stopped to watch a game of lawn-tennis, in which Octavia and Lord Lansdowne had joined, and finally forgot Lady Theobald's errand altogether.

For some time Octavia did not see him. She was playing with great spirit, and Lord Lansdowne was following her delightedly.

Finally a chance of the game bringing her to him, she turned suddenly, and found Barold's eyes fixed upon her.

"How long have you been there?" she asked.

"Some time," he answered. "When you are at liberty, I wish to speak to you."

"Do you?" she said.

She seemed a little unprepared for the repressed energy of his manner. which he strove to cover by a greater amount of coldness than usual.

"Well," she said, after thinking a moment, "the game will soon be ended. I am going through the conservatories with Lord Lansdowne in course of time; but I dare say he can wait."

She went back, and finished her game, apparently enjoying it as much as ever. When it was over, Barold made his way to her.

He had resented her remaining oblivious of his presence when he stood near her, and he had resented her enjoyment of her surroundings; and now, as he led her away, leaving Lord Lansdowne rather disconsolate, he resented the fact that she did not seem nervous, or at all impressed by his silence.

"What do you want to say to me?" she asked. "Let us go and sit down in one of the arbors. I believe I am a little tired — not that I mind it, though. I've been having a lovely time."

Then she began to talk about Lord Lansdowne.

"I like him ever so much," she said.

"Do you think he will really go to America? I wish he would; but if he does, I hope it won't be for a year or so — I mean, until we go back from Europe. Still, it's rather uncertain when we *shall* go back. Did I tell you I had persuaded aunt Belinda to travel with us? She's horribly frightened, but I mean to make her go. She'll get over being frightened after a little while."

Suddenly she turned, and looked at him.

"Why don't you say something?" she demanded. "What's the matter?"

"It is not necessary for me to say any thing."

She laughed.

"Do you mean because I am saying every thing myself? Well, I suppose I am. I am — awfully happy to-day, and can't help talking. It seems to make the time go."

Her face had lighted up curiously. There was a delighted excitement in her eyes, puzzling him.

"Are you so fond of your father as all that?"

She laughed again, — a clear, exultant laugh.

"Yes," she answered, "of course I am as fond of him as all that. It's quite natural, isn't it?"

"I haven't observed the same degree of enthusiasm in all the young ladies of my acquaintance," he returned dryly.

He thought such rapture disproportionate to the cause, and regarded it grudgingly.

They turned into an arbor; and Octavia sat down, and leaned forward on the rustic table. Then she turned her face up to look at the vines covering the roof.

"It looks rather spidery, doesn't it?" she remarked. "I hope it isn't; don't you?"

The light fell bewitchingly on her round little chin and white throat; and a bar of sunlight struck on her upturned eyes, and the blonde rings on her forehead.

"There is nothing I hate more than spiders," she said, with a little shiver, "unless," seriously, "it's caterpillars — and caterpillars I loathe."

Then she lowered her gaze, and gave her hat — a large white Rubens, all soft, curling feathers and satin bows — a charming tip over her eyes.

"The brim is broad," she said. "If any thing drops, I hope it will drop on it, instead of on me. Now, what did you want to say?"

He had not sat down, but stood leaning against the rustic wood-work. He looked pale, and was evidently trying to be cooler than usual.

"I brought you here to ask you a question."

"Well," she remarked, "I hope it's an important one. You look serious enough."

"It is important, — rather," he responded, with a tone of sarcasm. "You will probably go away soon?"

"That isn't exactly a question," she commented, "and it's not as important to you as to me."

He paused a moment, annoyed because he found it difficult to go on; annoyed because she waited with such undisturbed serenity. But at length he managed to begin again.

"I do not think you are expecting the question I am going to ask," he said. "I — do not think I expected to ask it myself, — until to-day. I do not know why — why I should ask it so awkwardly, and feel — at such a disadvantage. I brought you here to ask you — to marry me."

He had scarcely spoken four words before all her airy manner had taken flight, and she had settled herself down to listen. He had noticed this, and had felt it quite natural. When he stopped, she was looking straight into his face. Her eyes were singularly large and bright and clear.

"You did not expect to ask me to marry you?" she said. "Why didn't you?"

It was not at all what he had expected. He did not understand her manner at all.

"I — must confess," he said stiffly, "that I felt at first that there were — obstacles in the way of my doing so."

"What were the obstacles?"

He flushed, and drew himself up.

"I have been unfortunate in my mode of expressing myself," he said. "I told you I was conscious of my own awkwardness."

"Yes," she said quietly: "you have been unfortunate. That is a good way of putting it."

Then she let her eyes rest on the table a few seconds, and thought a little.

"After all," she said, "I have the consolation of knowing that you must have been very much in love with me. If you had not been very much in love with me, you would never have asked me to marry you. You would have considered the obstacles."

"I am very much in love with you," he said vehemently, his feelings getting the better of his pride for once. "However badly I may have expressed myself, I am very much in love with you. I have been wretched for days."

"Was it because you felt obliged to ask me to marry you?" she inquired.

The delicate touch of spirit in her tone and words fired him to fresh admiration, strange to say. It suggested to him possibilities he had not suspected hitherto. He drew nearer to her.

"Don't be too severe on me," he said — quite humbly, considering all things.

And he stretched out his hand, as if to take hers.

But she drew it back, smiling ever so faintly.

"Do you think I don't know what the

obstacles are?" she said. "I will tell you."

"My affection was strong enough to sweep them away," he said, "or I should not be here."

She smiled slightly again.

"I know all about them, as well as you do," she said. "I rather laughed at them at first, but I don't now. I suppose I'm 'impressed by their seriousness,' as aunt Belinda says. I suppose they *are* pretty serious — to you."

"Nothing would be so serious to me as that you should let them interfere with my happiness," he answered, thrown back upon himself, and bewildered by her logical manner. "Let us forget them. I was a fool to speak as I did. Won't you answer my question?"

She paused a second, and then answered, —

"You didn't expect to ask me to marry you," she said. "And I didn't expect you to" —

"But now" — he broke in impatiently.

"Now — I wish you hadn't done it."

"You wish" —

"You don't want *me*," she said. "You want somebody meeker, — somebody who would respect you very much, and obey you. I'm not used to obeying people."

"Do you mean also that you would not respect me? he inquired bitterly.

"Oh," she replied, "you haven't respected me much!"

"Excuse me" — he began, in his loftiest manner.

"You didn't respect me enough to think me worth marrying," she said. "I was not the kind of girl you would have chosen of your own will."

"You are treating me unfairly!" he cried.

"You were going to give me a great deal, I suppose — looking at it in your way," she went on; "but, if I *wasn't* exactly what you wanted, I had something to give too. I'm young enough to have a good many years to live; and I should have to live them with you, if I married you. That's something, you know."

He rose from his seat pale with wrath and wounded feeling.

"Does this mean that you refuse me?" he demanded, "that your answer is 'no'?"

She rose, too — not exultant, not confused, neither pale nor flushed. He had never seen her prettier, more charming, or more natural.

"It would have been 'no,' even if there hadn't been any obstacle," she answered.

"Then," he said, "I need say no more. I see that I have — humiliated myself in vain; and it is rather bitter, I must confess."

"It wasn't my fault," she remarked

He stepped back, with a haughty wave of the hand, signifying that she should pass out of the arbor before him.

She did so; but just as she reached the entrance, she turned, and stood for a second, framed in by the swinging vines and their blossoms.

"There's another reason why it should be 'no,' she said. "I suppose I may as well tell you of it. I'm engaged to somebody else."

CHAPTER XXVI.

"JACK."

THE first person they saw, when they reached the lawn, was Mr. Dugald Binnie, who had deigned to present himself, and was talking to Mr. Burmistone, Lucia, and Miss Belinda.

"I'll go to them," said Octavia. "Aunt Belinda will wonder where I have been."

But, before they reached the group, they were intercepted by Lord Lansdowne; and Barold had the pleasure of surrendering his charge, and watching her, with some rather sharp pangs, as she was borne off to the conservatories.

"What is the matter with Mr. Barold?" exclaimed Miss Pilcher. "Pray look at him."

"He has been talking to Miss Octavia Bassett, in one of the arbors," put in Miss Lydia Burnham. "Emily and I passed them a few minutes ago, and they were so absorbed that they did not see us. There is no knowing what has happened."

"Lydia!" exclaimed Mrs. Burnham, in stern reproof of such flippancy.

But, the next moment, she exchanged a glance with Miss Pilcher.

"Do you think" — she suggested. "Is it possible" —

"It really looks very like it," said Miss Pilcher; "though it is scarcely to be credited. See how pale and angry he looks."

Mrs. Burnham glanced toward him, and then a slight smile illuminated her countenance.

"How furious," she remarked cheerfully, "how furious Lady Theobald will be!"

Naturally, it was not very long before the attention of numerous other ladies was directed to Mr. Francis Barold. It was observed that he took no share in the festivities, that he did not regain his natural air of enviable indifference to his surroundings, — that he did not approach Octavia Bassett until all was over, and she was on the point of going home. What he said to her then, no one heard.

"I am going to London to-morrow. Good-by."

"Good-by," she answered, holding out her hand to him. Then she added quickly, in an under-tone, "You oughtn't to think badly of me. You won't, after a while."

As they drove homeward, she was rather silent, and Miss Belinda remarked it.

"I am afraid you are tired, Octavia," she said. "It is a pity that Martin should come, and find you tired."

"Oh! I'm not tired. I was only — thinking. It has been a queer day."

"A queer day, my dear!" ejaculated Miss Belinda. "I thought it a charming day."

"So it has been," said Octavia, which Miss Belinda thought rather inconsistent.

Both of them grew rather restless as they neared the house.

"To think," said Miss Belinda, "of my seeing poor Martin again!"

"Suppose," said Octavia nervously, as they drew up, "suppose they are here — already."

"They?" exclaimed Miss Belinda. "Who" — but she got no farther. A cry burst from Octavia, — a queer, soft little cry.

"They are here," she said: "they are! Jack — Jack!"

And she was out of the carriage; and Miss Belinda, following her closely, was horrified to see her caught at once in the embrace of a tall, bronzed young man, who, a moment after, drew her into the little parlor, and shut the door.

Mr. Martin Bassett, who was big and sunburned, and prosperous-looking, stood in the passage, smiling triumphantly.

"M — M — Martin!" gasped Miss Belinda. "What — oh, what does this mean?"

Martin Bassett led her to a seat, and smiled more triumphantly still.

"Never mind, Belinda," he said. "Don't be frightened. It's Jack Belasys, and he's the finest fellow in the West. And she hasn't seen him for two years."

"Martin," Miss Belinda fluttered, "it is not proper — it really isn't."

"Yes, it is," answered Mr. Bassett; "for he's going to marry her before we go abroad."

It was an eventful day for all parties concerned. At its close Lady Theobald found herself in an utterly bewildered and thunderstruck condition. And to Mr. Dugald Binnie, more than to any one else, her demoralization was due. That gentleman got into the carriage, in rather a better humor than usual.

"Same man I used to know," he remarked. "Glad to see him. I knew him as soon as I set eyes on him."

"Do you allude to Mr. Burmistone?"

"Yes. Had a long talk with him. He's coming to see you to-morrow. Told him he might come, myself. Appears he's taken a fancy to Lucia. Wants to talk it over. Suits me exactly, and suppose it suits her. Looks as if it does. Glad she hasn't taken a fancy to some haw-haw fellow, like that fool Barold. Girls generally do. Burmistone's worth ten of him."

Lucia, who had been looking steadily out of the carriage-window, turned, with an amazed expression. Lady Theobald had received a shock which made all her manacles rattle. She could scarcely support herself under it.

"Do I"—she said. "Am I to understand that Mr. Francis Barold does not meet with your approval?"

Mr. Binnie struck his stick sharply upon the floor of the carriage.

"Yes, by George!" he said. "I'll have nothing to do with chaps like that. If she'd taken up with him, she'd never have heard from *me* again. Make sure of that."

When they reached Oldclough, her ladyship followed Lucia to her room. She stood before her, arranging the manacles on her wrists nervously.

"I begin to understand now," she said. "I find I was mistaken in my impressions of Mr. Dugald Binnie's tastes—and in my impressions of *you*. You are to marry Mr. Burmistone. My rule is over. Permit me to congratulate you."

The tears rose to Lucia's eyes.

"Grandmamma," she said, her voice soft and broken, "I think I should have been more frank, if—if you had been kinder sometimes."

"I have done my duty by you," said my lady.

Lucia looked at her pathetically.

"I have been ashamed to keep things from you," she hesitated. "And I have often told myself that — that it was sly to do it — but I could not help it."

"I trust," said my lady, "that you will be more candid with Mr. Burmistone."

Lucia blushed guiltily.

"I — think I shall, grandmamma," she said.

It was the Rev. Alfred Poppleton who assisted the rector of St. James to marry Jack Belasys and Octavia Bassett; and it was observed that he was almost as pale as his surplice.

Slowbridge had never seen such a wedding, or such a bride as Octavia. It was even admitted that Jack Belasys was a singularly handsome fellow, and had a dashing, adventurous air, which carried all before it. There was a rumor that he owned silver-mines himself, and had even done something in diamonds, in Brazil, where he had spent the last two years. At all events, it was ascertained beyond doubt, that, being at last a married woman, and entitled to splendors of the kind, Octavia would not lack them. Her present to Lucia, who was one of her bridesmaids, dazzled all beholders.

When she was borne away by the train, with her father and husband, and Miss Belinda, whose bonnet-strings were bedewed with tears, the Rev. Alfred Poppleton was the last man who shook hands with her. He held in his hand a large bouquet, which Octavia herself had given him out of her abundance. "Slowbridge will miss you, Miss — Mrs. Belasys," he faltered. "I — I shall miss you. Perhaps we — may even meet again. I have thought that, perhaps, I should like to go to America."

And, as the train puffed out of the station and disappeared, he stood motionless for several seconds; and a large and brilliant drop of moisture appeared on the calyx of the lily which formed the centre-piece of his bouquet.